Dia has just moved to a new city to run her own hair salon. She doesn't have time for the hot guy who won't stop asking her out, yet she can't seem to stop thinking about him.

Stone Blaylock is the Battletown Packs' Alpha and his mate has just moved into town. Problem is, she's human. Therefore, he has to win her over the old fashioned, human way—by dating her.

Things are looking up for Stone when he gets his mate to fall in love with and mate him.

However, there's someone out there who doesn't like that the Alpha's new mate is human. When their plan to kill her backfires and Dia survives, but she doesn't remember anything, including Stone, or the circumstances that left her alone, hurt, and pregnant.

# *the* Alpha's
# Secret Family

## by
## Jessie Lane

Raves for the novels by

# JESSIE LANE

## *Big Bad Bite*

"If you like funny paranormal romance with crazy but endearing characters, Big Bad Bite will be for you."

**- Swept Away By Romance**

## *Walk On The Striped Side*

"…this series is building to be a go to for PNR fans!"

**- Little Read Riding Hood**

"Seriously y'all if you're looking for a fun and sexy paranormal romance you need to pick up Walk On The Striped Side, I'll never look at cat toys the same way… Fans of Shelly Laurenston and Jessica Sims will fall in love with Jessie Lane's Big Bad Bite series."

**- The Book Nympho**

### *Lone Wolf Wanted*

"Jessie Lane writes fun, sexy characters with a bit of sass."

**- Patricia A. Rasey, national bestselling author**

### *Bears Do It Better*

"This is my first book by Jessie Lane and most definitely will not be my last. I have not laughed this hard at a book in a while. The quirky humor was great."

**- Reading in Sarah's Corner**

### *Sassy and a little Bad-Assy*

"Absolutely hysterical! Really enjoyed the playfulness of the characters and their word play. While not completely comedic it had just the right amount of emotion to make both H/h feel real. I do love my HEA's. Thank you Ms. Lane for bringing a little laughter to my day."

**- Amazon Reviewer**

# The Alpha's Secret Family

By Jessie Lane

Edited by: Read Head Editing, C&D Editing &
Shannon Webb
Cover Design by: Jessie Lane
Cover Images by: © Clarissa at Yocla | Volodymyr
Tverdokhlib | Shutterstock

**For more information on Jessie Lane:**

http://jessielanebooks.com

**Or you can send Jessie Lane an email at:**

jessie_lane@jessielanebooks1.com

# Other Titles From Jessie Lane

## *Ex Ops Series*
Secret Maneuvers
Stripping Her Defenses
Mission Delivery
Sweet Agony
Sweet Recovery
Sweet Eternity
Bullets and Bluebonnets

## *Regulators MC Series*
*(co-written with Chelsea Camaron)*
Ice
Hammer
Coal

## *Big Bad Bite Series*
Big Bad Bite
Walk On The Striped Side

## *Star Series*
*(co-written with M.L. Pahl)*
The Burning Star
The Frozen Star

## *Standalone Stories*
The Alpha's Secret Family

## *Kindle World Stories*
Lone Wolf Wanted
Sassy and a little Bad-Assy
Bears Do It Better

# The Alpha's Secret Family

*by*

## Jessie Lane

# Dedication

*To my readers. I am sincerely grateful for each and*

*every one of you.*

*Love, Jessie Lane*

# Acknowledgements

There are a few ladies I want to thank for helping me with this book: Abbie Zanders, Chelsea Camaron and Heather Ray. Thank you so much ladies! I'd also like to say another huge thank you to my editors Read Head Editing, C&D Editing and Shannon Webb. I don't know what I would do without you three.

# *Prologue*

*Thank God for my favorite "f" word—Friday.* That was all Dia could think as she walked into the first restaurant she could find after leaving her new job for the day.

She walked into the Battletown Diner and asked the hostess for a table for one. The pretty brunette standing at the counter gave her a fake smile and guided her toward one of the tables in the back. Not that it bothered Dia. No, she wanted peace and quiet after a hard day at work.

What had she been thinking, moving hours away from her family in Nashville to buy out a hair salon from her former mentor? Sure, she loved Betty Anne to pieces, and the woman had taught her everything she knew, but after begging her for a job five years ago, Betty Anne had been the one begging somebody to take over her own little salon so she could retire, and that person had been Dia. Now she lived out in the middle of nowhere!

There was farmland everywhere she looked. And she had seen more cows in the past week than she had thought was possible. Seriously, how many cows did it take to make a gallon of milk, anyway? Because with the number of cows she had seen in and around Battletown, the rivers should be made of milk. This was probably what lactose intolerant people considered hell.

The small town was bustling with locals, but it wasn't a major city with tons of potential clients. She was worried that perhaps she should have turned down Betty Anne's amazing offer and stayed in the city near her parents. Except, if she had done that, what would her future look like? Always working for someone else in their salon instead of owning her own? Real estate in the city was expensive. There was no way she would have ever been able to afford her own shop in Nashville. It would have taken a lot of big spenders as clients to ever work up that kind of cash, and Dolly Parton wasn't exactly knocking down her door to get her hair done. So, Dia's best chance of owning her own shop was here with Betty Anne's already established clients.

As Dia sat at her table looking at the laminated dinner menu, her mind swirled with doubts and worries. So much so, that she wasn't reading the menu at all, just lost in her thoughts. All of that changed when the chair across from her scraped across the floor as it was dragged backward and someone sat down.

Suddenly, every nerve ending and instinct in Dia's body flared to life. Although she hadn't looked up yet, she somehow knew two things. One, it was a man. The spicy scent of him wafted across the table and filled her senses until her head spun. And two, for some odd reason, her entire being knew that her life was about to change forever.

How weird was that?

Not only weird, but scary. Dia's life had already changed so much in the last few days with her move to town and taking over the business. There was no way she was ready for it to change any more.

She tried to ignore the unknown man, hoping he might go away if she paid him no attention. Just minutes later, though, she found out that wasn't going to work, as he leaned forward and braced his arms on the table.

"You going to ignore me all night, princess?"

The unknown man's voice was so deliciously deep that it tingled certain parts of her body. She loved a deep bass like that. His voice wasn't what made her head snap up, though. No, it was her irritation.

"I'm not a fucking princess," she snapped back.

She hated when people made assumptions about her just because of the way she looked. Just because she liked to have her make-up and hair done at all times didn't mean that she was a high-maintenance woman. Dia could swing a hammer just as good as any guy in here, and if the stranger didn't watch it, she would swing that hammer at his head.

It didn't take much to set off Dia's fiery temper.

Of course, the urge to hit him abruptly died away when she got her first good look at the man she had studiously tried to avoid only seconds before. The word beautiful didn't seem to do the man justice. No, he was absolutely and utterly beard-bodacious beautiful.

He had dark, shaggy hair she immediately wanted to run her fingers through, and gorgeous steel-grey eyes. His facial features were strong, like his jaw, and undoubtedly handsome. Rugged was how one might describe them. Not Dia, though. No, the word predatory was the word that came to mind as she looked at his intent eyes and the smirk on his lips. The man was staring at her like he was a starving wolf and she was the plump, little lamb he had set his sights on.

Would it be terribly wrong if she gave in to temptation and asked him to eat her? Because looking at the stranger made her hotter than any other man had before. He was just that damn devastating. The realization made Dia feel confused because she had never had this sort of reaction to a man before.

The stranger's smirk spread into a huge grin as he watched her after she snapped the heated words at him.

She waited for his rebuttal; some condescension that she hadn't needed to be so snippety. Instead, he leaned forward and whispered, "All right, sweetheart, I get it; you're not a princess. I just couldn't help myself because, here you sit, in this little restaurant, surrounded by farmers and working men, prettier than anything I've ever seen in my whole life. You haven't noticed that every single man's eyes are glued to you, and you haven't seen their pitiful attempts to get your attention. So, I had to come over here and make sure you had no choice but to notice me."

"Why is that?" she asked him curiously.

"Because you're mine."

Dia's eyebrows shot up to her hairline. "Ugh, you might not want to come on so strongly, buddy."

"As you wish."

Oh boy, Dia suddenly had the overwhelming feeling that she was in serious trouble with this guy. She just hoped it was the good time sort of trouble.

# *Chapter One*

*One week later...*

"I told him his dick was so small that it looked like a California raisin."

The two clients in Dia's shop started giggling at the story one told the other about catching their cheating boyfriend in the act. Dia knew the sting of that sort of situation, as it had happened to her in the past.

She smiled at the women's conversation as she trimmed the client's ends on her angled bob. The women had come in that day, stating they wanted makeovers, and now Dia knew why. There was nothing like giving the proverbial middle finger to an ex-boyfriend, then stepping out the next day, looking better than you had while you were dating. For that reason alone, Dia wanted to make sure that she had every strand cut to perfection. That was probably why it caught her off guard when they asked her a question.

"Miss Dia, I hear you've got a sexy man at your beck and call these days," her client's friend said in a teasing voice.

Dia tried not to blush, but failed. Damn her pale skin!

Shrugging as if to play it off, she admitted to the women, "He's certainly persistent."

"Giiiiiiirl," her client sang out in the chair. "You have no idea how juicy this gossip is. Stone Blaylock hasn't ever chased a woman. Now you move to town, and he's on you like a dog is on a bone. The whole town is talking about it."

"Dog with a bone, eh?" Her friend laughed. "If that man is a dog, then he can give me a tongue bath anytime, and then I want to play with his bone."

The two women burst into giggles all over again. Only, Dia didn't smile at them this time. Something inside of her didn't like the idea of other women fantasizing about Stone. It was an irrational feeling, but damn if she could help herself. The confusion her emotions brought kept her mind busy as she finished up her client's cut, and then checked the women out of her salon.

Glancing at the clock, Dia saw time had flown by, and it was already five o'clock, which meant it was time to start closing the salon for the night.

She was almost done with her routine, sweeping the floor one last time, when she started to think about the Stone. The man was impossible. Every day her little salon had been open he had come in to see her. The first time was for a haircut and to ask her out on a date. She had given him a trim and told him no on the date. Then she had charged him double what she normally would for a men's cut just to be a pain in his ass. That hadn't stopped the man from coming back, though.

Every day, he asked the same question: "Will you go out with me tonight?"

Every day, for six days straight, Dia had given him the same answer: "No."

And just before he would leave, Stone would say the same thing: "As you wish, princess."

The first time he had said that to her, she had flipped him the bird. The second time, because there hadn't been anyone in the shop to see her do it, she had thrown a comb at his head. The man had simply ducked the flying arsenal and laughed at her. The third time he called her princess, she had been ready to rip both his and her own hair out in a frustrated rage. By the fourth day, however, she couldn't help wondering why not? Even after he had shown up and she had once again told him "no," she had found herself thinking about him after he had left.

Why did he come in every day to ask the same question, knowing he was probably going to get the same answer? And why did he insist on calling her "princess?" It had to be because he knew it drove her crazy.

What he didn't know was, by the fifth day, it had also made her smile after he left. The man had the balls to say it to her every day, and apparently, she liked that in a man more than she had realized. So much so, that later that night, while she had been lying in bed, she had started to think about him. His gorgeous smile and pretty eyes. How his rugged features made him stand out in a crowd. It was then that Dia had decided that, if Stone came back for more than a week, she would give in and let him take her out on a date.

Now it was day seven, and Dia was nervous. Would Stone come by again? Or had he taken all of her noes to heart and given up on her? It wasn't until now, at the thought of losing his attention, that Dia realized just how much she had come to crave it. And here it was, five-thirty and Stone had yet to come by for the day.

Disheartened that she had scared away the man who had become the object of her fascination, Dia turned out the lights, walked out the front door, and locked her salon up for the night.

Completely preoccupied with her thoughts and feeling sort of sad, she turned and started walking toward her car, her eyes on the ground. That probably why, as she walked around the front of her car, she didn't see the car flying toward her down the busy street.

Tires squealed, catching her attention. She turned her head just in time to see a black Jeep racing straight toward her. Truly, it was only ten feet or so from hitting her, and she knew she was probably about to die.

That didn't stop her from turning and throwing herself in the direction she had just come from, but as she felt something hit her hard, she realized it was too late. She hadn't moved fast enough to get out of the Jeep's path.

Her back hit the hood of her car and a heavy weight slammed down on top of her as she heard the Jeep rev its engine and drive on. Dia listened to the vehicle as it disappeared into the distance, unwilling to open her eyes. The weight on top of her was so heavy she figured it was probably a piece of the Jeep that had broken off. With her luck, it would probably crush her to death. She figured it would be better if she just laid there and hoped she died quickly.

A few silent minutes passed, and then the heavy weight on top of her shifted, just plain freaking her the fuck out! How could a piece of car laying on top of you move when you were lying still?

"Are you just going to lie there all night?"

Her eyes popped open in shock at the rumbly voice that had spoken to her, and she gasped.

There was Stone, not some piece of a Jeep, holding her down on the hood of her car. Now that she was paying attention, she could feel every hard muscle of his body pressing against hers. His legs were straddling her, lining his body up with hers perfectly, his manhood snug against her core.

Honestly, Dia didn't know whether to laugh or cry. Part of her wanted to laugh because the very man she had been thinking about was on top of her. The other part of her wanted to cry because she had thought she was going to be a goner there for a second. Thanks to the man staring down at her, she was going to keep breathing long enough to try out that red hair dye she had been eyeing for the last year.

Dia was just about to thank Stone, but in true annoying man fashion, he opened his mouth and said, "You know, I just saved your life."

"Yes, and I'm very grateful for that," she told him honestly. "Now, can you please get off me? I think we should probably call the police. Whoever that was in the Jeep was driving like a maniac!"

Stone didn't move a muscle. Instead, he asked, "Will you go out with me now?"

The question made her queasy stomach flip, which wasn't really a good thing at the moment.

"You're not going to give up, are you?" Dia asked, trying to push down the urge to be sick. It wasn't that she had second thoughts about going out with Stone; it was the knowledge that she had almost just bit the dust! And here he was, lying on top of her and asking her out for a date!

He brought his head down until they were nose to nose. "On you, princess? Never."

That temper of hers flared to life. "I just almost died! Are you kidding me? Get off me, you ass, so I can call the cops!"

"Not until you agree to go out with me."

"Have you lost your fucking mind?" she yelled angrily at him.

Stone, however, wasn't the least bit bothered by Dia's anger. He just kept staring at her as he said, "Well, are you going to go out with me now or what? I can lie here like this all night, princess."

"Yes!" Dia shouted in frustration. "Yes, I'll go out with you! Now, please get off me."

Stone slid down her body until his feet hit the ground, and then he grabbed her hand and pulled her up.

The moment Dia's feet hit the ground, she was looking through her purse for her cell phone. And the second she whipped it out, Stone grabbed it from her.

"You won't be needing that, sweetheart."

Giving him an incredulous look, Dia asked, "Why the hell not?"

He nodded toward the direction the Jeep had disappeared. "That was old woman Jones. She's almost ninety years old and drives to the grocery store once a week. Problem is, she has a lead foot, and I suspect she's blind as a bat. She probably never saw you standing there. Now, you wouldn't want to put an old lady in jail, would you?"

Dia's jaw dropped open as she realized what he had just done. "You tricked me into a date."

The infuriating man had the nerve to smile at her. "I'll do what I have to do to get what I want. Keep that in mind, princess." Handing her phone back, Stone then turned away and headed toward his truck, whistling.

Dia watched him open the door and climb in, still too shocked at his devious ploy to say anything else.

Before he closed the door, he looked back to her and winked. "See you tomorrow for lunch, princess." Then the man shut his truck door and drove away like he hadn't just turned her entire world upside down.

*Damn men!* If he hadn't just saved her life, she would totally Taser his nuts.

# *Chapter Two*

***One week later…***

"I want you to make me a strawberry blonde, but I don't want you to use any red, orange, or gold hair dyes. Just the strawberry and the blonde."

Dia looked at her new client with what she hoped wasn't murder in her eyes. Why was it that women always thought they could come in here and ask the impossible of her? Did she look like some sort of wish-granting genie? Since she was wearing her normal black dress pants, a cute top, her favorite heels, with her hair and makeup done, she would have to say that, no, she did not look like a freaking genie. Unless there was an alternate world where genies looked like super curvy, hairstyling Barbie dolls.

She couldn't just haul off and let the woman have it, though, so she tried to be nice about it. Miss Dempey—"

"That's *Mrs.* Dempey, young lady," her client told her with a disdainful sniff.

Dia's temper flared, and she had to silently chant to herself not to cut a bald spot on the woman's head.

Clearing her mind, she tried again. "Mrs. Dempey, there is no way I can make you a strawberry blonde without using red, gold, or orange. Especially the red. Hence the strawberry in the blonde."

Outraged, the uppity woman stood up from the chair. "You're just as incompetent as Betty Anne was! I'll just have to drive into Louisville to get my hair done by *real* professionals."

At the end of her tirade, the customer stormed out, leaving Dia seething in her wake. What she wouldn't give to put some hair remover in that woman's shampoo bottle.

Left in the shop with no appointments scheduled for the rest of her day, Dia took one look at the clock, saw it was three in the afternoon, and thought, *Fuck it. I'm closing the salon early and going home.*

In a foul mood, she started the process of closing. When she was down to sweeping the floors for the last time that day, her mind turned back to the man it thought of a little too much these days—Stone.

A week ago, she had given in to temptation and decided to let the man try to woo her. It might have sounded old fashioned, but that was only because Dia had grown up with two parents who were madly in love with each other. Her mom had always told her that she needed to wait for a man who made her body tingle from head to toe. Her father had said she needed to wait for a man that she couldn't stop thinking about. It seemed Stone fit both of those criteria.

Since making that decision, she and Stone had been out on five dates. He had taken her out to lunch one day, dinner the next, and to a movie on the third night. He had held her hand, opened every door, and had paid for everything. She was starting to wonder if he was the perfect gentleman, up to the fourth date when he punched a man out for whistling at her ass as she walked by the man's table.

That was when Dia realized Stone wasn't just a gentleman; he was an alpha man. And she meant that in the best way. Stone was the sort of man to pound his chest and let the world know she was his woman. He wasn't going to let anyone else look at, or even think about, what he considered his.

The question Dia had now was simple: Did she want to be Stone's woman? The man was making it plain as day that was what he considered her. It was obvious in every protective, territorial move he made. The way he placed his hand at the small of her back when they were walking somewhere. How he kissed her breathless every chance she gave him. Even the way he checked her little apartment over the salon every night to make sure it was safe before he kissed her good night then left.

The man was a walking, talking caveman … and she was really starting to like it.

Dia was just finishing up sweeping when she heard the bell over her front door ring. She turned her head to see who was coming in and had to bite her lip not to smile. Every time she saw him now, Dia's heart would skip a beat and other parts of her would tingle. The man was the epitome of butterflies in her stomach. Sex on a stick. Tall, dark, and sinfully handsome.

To put it mildly, Stone had become her shot of mantastic love drug, and she had quickly becoming addicted to him.

"Hey, handsome, what are you doing here?"

Stone stopped only a few inches from her. She could smell the cinnamon gum he had been chewing. Mmmmm … she loved cinnamon. That would make it fun to kiss him later.

That wasn't what held her attention, though. No, it was his eyes. There was something about them today that was different. She just couldn't quite put her finger on it. It was almost as if he was anxious or something.

"You have any more clients today?"

Dia shook her head.

"Will you come out with me, then? I have a surprise for you, but I warn you, it's a bit of a drive."

Leaning on the broom, Dia cocked her hip to the side and put her hand on it. "How far of a drive?"

"Two hours. Think you can make it that far, princess?"

She had gotten used to him calling her the nickname, but it didn't mean she liked it.

Deciding to be sarcastic, Dia said, "Don't know, handsome, might be too far. If we are out past my bedtime, I turn into a pumpkin."

Stone leaned forward until their mouths almost touched. "What if I told you it was worth staying up past your bedtime?"

Her breath hitched at his innuendo. Was she ready to get handsy with the hunk she had been seeing?

Stone leaned forward and ran his nose along hers, before giving her a small, enticing kiss on the mouth. Then he pulled back and whispered, "Come with me."

"Ever heard of the word please?" she whispered back, trying to sass him.

He shook his head, and she giggled as he wrapped an arm around Dia's waist and brought their bodies flush together. It was then that his eyes pleaded with her as he said again, "Come with me."

Dia felt that same feeling she had back at the diner when she had first met Stone. As if this moment was important, and her whole life was about to change. It sounded crazy to think that, but she couldn't help it. So now the question was: Did she take a chance on the caveman and the crazy feeling?

Fuck it. Hadn't that been what she had been doing since she told Betty Ann she would move to Battletown and take over the salon?

Dia took a big breath for courage. "Lead the way, Prince Charming."

Stone cocked his head to the side instead of moving like she thought he would. "And what if I said I was the big bad wolf instead of Prince Charming? Would you run from me, then?"

Dia bit her bottom lip nervously. "What if I told you I thought wolves were cute and furry, so even you, the big bad wolf, couldn't make me run away?"

Stone answered her cryptically, "Let's hope you're right." Then, without giving her a chance to say another word, he pulled her out the door, only stopping long enough to let her lock up.

The next two hours and five minutes were spent in his truck, traveling the roads to wherever the surprise was. They sat in companionable silence, Dia curled up against Stone's side on the bench seat as he drove. For a while, she thought he might be taking her to Lexington, based on the highway signs, but when she asked him if that was their destination, he told her no.

Finally, just before they would hit Lexington, in the town of Versailles, Stone asked her to close her eyes. Dia almost asked him why, then decided to let the man have his surprise. She had a feeling giving in just this once was going to be worth it.

She took one last long look at him, then gave him her trust by closing her eyes.

"Thank you, princess."

Feeling playful, Dia reminded him, "I'm not a fucking princess," to which he laughed.

When they stopped, Stone gently pulled her out of the truck, then hauled her up into his arms. "Hold on tight, sweetheart. This won't take long."

She felt him walk away from the truck and heard his steps in the grass beneath his boots. Her arms were wrapped around his neck, so she took the opportunity to put her nose at the spot between his shoulder and neck, inhaling his natural spicy scent. Stone gave her a little growl, and she couldn't help laughing at the sound.

Dia had no idea how long Stone carried her to their destination, but just when she was about to say something to him about putting her down because she didn't want to break his back before they could have sex, Stone finally stopped.

Setting her gently on her feet, his deep voice rumbled, "Ready?"

Dia was breathless with anticipation as she felt Stone move behind her, setting his hands on her hips before placing his mouth next to the shell of her ear.

"Open your eyes, princess." What she saw next took her breath away. It was a castle—in freaking Kentucky!

It was made of stone with several turrets, and even from a distance, she could see it was two generous levels tall. The sun was setting behind it, the sky a red and peach flow, in stark contrast to the lavender clouds. It was by far the most beautiful thing she had seen in her entire life.

Stone's deep voice rumbled softly next to her ear. "Thought I could bring my princess to see a castle sunset."

"I'm not a fucking princess," she whispered back, still in awe.

He laughed, then buried his face in her neck. Mumbling against her skin, he said the three words she was getting oh so used to hearing him say. "As you wish."

"This is like a fairy tale," Dia told him, still staring at the glorious sight before them.

Stone's body went rock hard with tension behind her, and his grip tightened on her hips, almost to the point of pain. "And do you believe in fairy tales, Dia?"

Prying his hands off her, she turned and wrapped her arms around his neck. "These days, I think I do."

"And what if I told you I was something straight out of a fairy tale, would you believe me?"

Thinking he was teasing, Dia teased back, "Is this where you tell me you really are Prince Charming?"

When Stone didn't laugh at her joke, Dia took notice of the tension in the air around them and stiffened herself.

"Or, are you the frog under those clothes?"

He grabbed her tightly, almost as if he was afraid she would ask him to let her go. "I'm not Prince Charming, sweetheart."

"Then what are you talking about?" Dia asked him, confused.

"I'm the big bad wolf, Dia."

She started to laugh, thinking he was joking again, but his serious face stopped her.

Quickly getting confused and frustrated with his mood swings, she snapped, "Fine, if you're such a big bad wolf, then how about you prove it to me, then? Do something … wolfy."

One of his eyebrows cocked up. "*Wolfy?*"

Dia nodded, determined to straighten out this confusing mess. She had no idea what the hell Stone was trying to get at here, but she wasn't one for bullshit. It was best just to cut right through the crap.

Crossing her arms over her chest, she reiterated her command, "Wolfy, mister."

Shrugging his shoulders, Stone started to move, but not in any way she had expected him to. No, the crazy man started stripping his clothes off.

"What the hell are you doing, Stone?" Dia glanced around, worried someone might see him getting naked.

With a laugh in his voice, Stone answered her as he pushed his boots off his feet, "I'm getting wolfy, woman. Give me a minute, would ya?"

Tired of the man acting like a total lunatic, Dia put a hand over her eyes to block the sight of him and shouted, "You will put your clothes back on right this minute, Stone Blaylock, or I will never speak to you again!"

Stone didn't answer her with words ... There were grunts. Then a long groan. Followed by ... a growl?

Past the point of confusion, and a whole lot worried, Dia peeked between two of her fingers to where Stone should have been standing. But he wasn't there. That was when Dia removed her hand altogether and looked to find a massive wolf in his place.

Dia's fear and adrenaline kicked in right away. She had good reason to be scared, too. The damn wolf was almost twice the size of any wolf she had seen at a zoo, and licking his chops like she was dinner.

She started to take a step back, but that made the wolf growl at her. She froze in place, staring down at an animal who could rip her apart from limb to limb.

The wolf didn't move a muscle, just stood there staring at her, as if he wanted her to see something. It took her a while, probably because she was ready to pee her pants, but Dia finally did see something. Steel blue-gray eyes, the exact same shade as Stone's.

It was as if the wolf knew the moment she had picked up that bit of knowledge, because his mouth spread into a big, wolf grin that flashed all of his sharp teeth.

Dia didn't have time to think or say anything about those eyes or teeth, though, because then something unbelievable happened. The wolf started moving, and not as in moving toward her or away from her. No, the body started changing. Fur receded into skin, the body elongated, and the next thing she knew, there was a very naked Stone standing in front of her, watching for her reaction.

The thing was, Dia was feeling so many different emotions she wasn't sure what reaction to give the man. Or wolf. Or whatever the fuck he was.

They stood there, silently staring at each other for a few minutes, until Stone asked, "Well? You going to say anything?"

Dia opened her mouth … then shut it again. In fact, she did that a few times, making herself look like a gaping fish, until she realized she was in genuine shock.

No matter how hard she tried, no words would come out.

Stone seemed to realize her predicament and stepped closer to her. Holding a hand out, he used one finger to slide it down the side of her face in a gentle caress. "Go ahead and say it, princess. Say the words: 'You're a shifter'."

Finally, words came out when she opened her mouth, but they weren't the words he wanted her to say.

"You're not a werewolf?"

Stone shook his head. "We go by the name shifter, not werewolf."

"Not a werewolf," Dia said, instead of asking this time.

"Not a werewolf," Stone repeated.

After that, Dia could only think of one thing she wanted to ask him. "Do you get fleas?"

Stone wasn't thrilled with her question and let her know it with a look. "Not funny, mate."

"Mate?" Dia squeaked.

Nodding, he repeated, "Mate."

That was about the time Dia passed out.

# *Chapter Three*

*Two months later…*

"I don't want you to go."

The growly man watching her from the bed made her smile.

Dia stood there, watching him through the mirror as she ran the brush through her strawberry blonde tresses to get the tangles out that her growly man had helped put in only moments before. She was in nothing but his T-shirt after they had just finished making love a few minutes ago.

While she knew it would be smarter not to play with a brooding alpha wolf shifter, Dia just couldn't help herself. Her man was cranky, and she was half-naked and content. That was certainly a recipe for mischief, right?

To do this, Dia made sure she moved her weight from foot to foot every now and then between brushings so that her mate, Stone, would watch what he knew was her bare ass moving underneath the clothing as she spoke with him.

"I know you don't want me to go, love, but you know I have to." She looked over her shoulder at her frowning mate and smiled. "Besides, Stone, I haven't seen my family since we met and mated two months ago. My parents are ready to send the cops out to make sure I really am okay and not being held hostage by some man they've never met. If I make an appearance so they can see I really am okay, they'll feel better. Plus, Mom needs me to help her after the knee surgery she's about to have. Not to mention all the trouble I've gone to, working double-time to cover my clients so I could close the salon and take this time off. I'll be back in a couple of weeks."

"I'll have someone checking on the salon while you're gone."

"Thank you, handsome," Dia told him with a big grin. She knew that admission meant he was slowly giving in to her leaving.

She looked back toward the mirror, started brushing her hair again, and gave her butt another surreptitious wiggle. She could barely hold in her laugh when she saw the movement had immediately gained Stone's attention. Then she heard him growl.

"You're trying to distract me on purpose, woman."

At that comment, a giggle escaped her, and she watched through the mirror as his head snapped up and he glared at her.

"You should know better than to play with a wolf."

Oh, she had learned that, and many other things about shifters in her time with her mate. Just saying the word mate in her head still made her heart flutter in her chest a little. She couldn't believe how far they had come in such a short period of time. From strangers to soul mates in just a matter of months. But that was how shifters were.

According to Stone, they knew their true mate immediately. It was hard to believe, but with every minute she had spent with him after that day by the castle, Stone had shown her the truth of his claim. There was no doubt in her mind that she was his mate, and that he loved her more than anything else in the world.

Dia had fallen hard and fast, and she wasn't looking back. Not that she would want to. This whole "mate" thing was pretty cool. What woman didn't want a smokin' hot man who wanted to love, protect, and basically worship the ground she walked on? Plus, the sex! She wasn't sure if all shifters were as voracious as Stone, but if they were, all of woman-kind would be searching for a shifter mate. That reminded Dia … She still had a little time to fool around with her mate before she left. What girl wouldn't take that opportunity?

She gave her ass another little wiggle, knowing he was staring at it. Then she had to bite the inside of her cheek not to laugh at the growl she heard from behind her.

Looking back at Stone through the mirror again, she saw the grumpy man she had quickly grown to love more than life itself throw the sheet off his naked body, and then got out of the bed. What a glorious naked body it was. To her, it was the epitome of perfection.

Stone was tall, well over six feet, and built with lots of lean muscles. That shaggy hair she loved to run her fingers through and would never cut short, complimented his beautiful eyes. He also had a strong, square jaw that helped to accentuate his plump bottom lip. It might seem silly, but she really loved that lip. Or biting it, at least.

And her favorite body part on Stone? It was hanging limp between his legs, its long length starting to harden with every step he took in her direction.

Her mate walked up behind where she stood in front of their long dresser and mirror, wrapped his hands around her waist, and hugged her tight. "I don't want you to travel without me. What if something happens to you? I won't be there to help."

Dia couldn't help smiling. Her mate worried over her constantly because she was human … and he was not.

Lifting a hand to her shoulder, he brushed his thumb over the scar there where he had bitten her and marked her as his forever.

Turning so that she faced him, Dia cradled his face in her hands. "Don't worry so much, Stone. You seem to forget that I managed to survive just fine before I met you. Trust me; I'll be fine, and it's only for a little while. If you didn't have the neighboring pack delegates arriving tomorrow, then you could come with me, but we both know you need to stay. I promise to call you every night."

"No, not good enough. I want you to call me three times a day."

Dia didn't bother to hide her laughing smile. Life had certainly become interesting with a man who was always used to getting his way. The word negotiation didn't seem to be in his vocabulary sometimes, but this time, she needed him to give in a little.

"I'll call you twice a day, Mr. Bossy, and not one call more. I'm there to spend time with my family, and I can't spend all the time on the phone with you."

If it were possible for a grown man to pout like a two-year-old, that was what Stone did. He definitely didn't like her answer.

"I think I need to convince you that three phone calls a day are absolutely necessary." Leaning forward, he nipped her bottom lip, and then kissed away the sting. Pulling back so that only their foreheads were touching, he grumbled, "Why do I have to stay here again?"

Dia giggled at the look on his face. He looked like he was a kid whose favorite toy had been taken away from him. "Because you're the alpha."

Stone leaned his head to the side and used that wicked tongue of his to lick from her shoulder up her neck. She moaned when the lick turned into a small, playful bite.

"Stop trying to keep me from going."

Her mate started walking backward toward their bed as he pulled her along with him. "How about I just remind you what you're going to be missing, mate?" Stone wrapped his hands around her waist and picked her up off the floor as he turned around to face the bed.

Dia wrapped her legs around his waist in return, rubbing herself on what was now his very hard length trapped between them.

Leaning his head down, he took her mouth in a hungry kiss that stole her breath. Playful nips to her lips, skillful movements of his tongue in and out of her mouth, all of it overwhelming her bit by bit.

Slowly, he then lowered her to the bed until her back was touching the soft pillowtop mattress, her legs still wrapped around his waist.

Pulling back from their kiss, with a husky voice, he asked, "Slow or fast, mate?"

"Slow, handsome. You gave me wild wolfman last round."

He dropped his face so that his nose could skim her neck and murmured, "Slow it is, then." Pushing her shirt up to bare her abdomen, Stone looked down her body and growled again. "Have I told you lately how much I love your body?"

Dia nodded. "About ten minutes ago, love."

"Ten minutes too long, then." He pulled out of her embrace so that he could skim his nose over her vulnerable belly. Then he licked it with his tongue, circling her belly button. "I love your body. It's perfect, and I want to kiss every inch of it."

"Every inch?" she gasped.

He nodded. "Every inch, sweetheart."

Feeling a bit devious again, Dia whispered, "How about you kiss a certain spot a little lower?" She bit her bottom lip as a big smile spread across his face.

"As you wish, mate."

With that, Stone dropped to his knees at the end of the bed and grabbed her by her hips to drag her body closer to him until her core was right there for him. She could already feel the warm breath from his mouth as he started inching closer to her throbbing center, making the anticipation of his touch seem torturous. When he finally did kiss her there, Dia gasped at the sensation. Stone knew just how to touch her to drive her wild. It was as if he was in tune with her every need.

He kissed her clit, then circled it with his tongue. Going straight for the sensitive spot was a shock, but a pleasant one. It wasn't long before he was licking her in firm strokes, driving her mad with want for him to be inside of her.

"I need you, Stone."

At her words, he stopped. "You have me, Dia, always."

She reached down and grabbed the sides of his face, gently pulling up so he would follow her unspoken directions. Stone settled himself between her thighs, brushing his hard, long length against her core, causing her to gasp and arch into him for more.

"Please, love," she begged him.

Stone lowered his face until their foreheads touched. He wanted to surround himself in the intimacy of this moment between himself and the one he loved; soak it up until it was embedded into his being. She fulfilled both him and his wolf like nobody else ever could.

"Please what, sweetheart?" he asked her.

Dia reached up so she could kiss him, delving her tongue in his mouth to swirl with his. Then she pulled back. "Please fill me up with you. When I leave here, I want to feel you for days. Every time I sit, walk, or move, I want to feel the memory of you inside of me."

A growl of pure need escaped him, and he used his hips to position himself at her opening. With one long, slow thrust, he filled her completely as she gasped out his name in pleasure. Then, when he was seated to the hilt, he asked, "Do you feel me now, sweetheart?"

"Yes," she gasped.

"Do you want to feel more?" he asked.

"I want to feel everything, Stone."

"As you wish, mate."

Stone started moving in and out of Dia. Long, slow, but firm thrusts with his eyes locked on her own. Setting a steady rhythm that drove her higher and higher until tears of happiness were slipping from her eyes, and even Stone's eyes were darkening with emotion. It didn't take long before he was pushing her over the crest of ecstasy. Plummeting her physically into an orgasm so strong, her entire body was trembling with the effects of it.

Dia grabbed Stone's shoulders with both hands, digging her nails into his skin as she became overwhelmed with both pleasure and the love she had for the man inside of her.

It was then, as she dug her nails into him, that she saw his eyes flash his wolf's amber glow, letting her know the animal was here as much as the man was, right before Stone ripped the shoulder of her shirt open with his right hand to bare the skin there. Before she knew it, he was biting her again on her mate mark, and her pleasure became more than she could handle.

Dia cried out blissfully, loving the feel of Stone surrounding her, inside of her, in every way that mattered, from his cock to his teeth. Making her his in all ways. She couldn't imagine life without him in moments like these.

Stone's tempo sped up a little. His thrusts became stronger until she could feel his long length tapping against the opening of her womb. She was too full, but damn it felt good. He thrusted just like that, giving her that overwhelmingly full feeling once, twice, and then on the third, he pulled his teeth from her shoulder and roared his release.

Dia could feel his spurts inside of her, the warmth of his seed spreading and filling her as he stopped moving above her and held his position, twitching with his own pleasure.

When her mate was done, he collapsed on top of her, making sure to keep his weight from crushing her. Then Stone gave her another long, leisurely kiss full of all the emotion she knew he felt for her. When they were breathless, he fell to his back and rolled her so that she lay on his chest.

As quiet fell around them, Stone whispered, "I'm going to miss you too fucking much, Dia. I'm not sure if I'll be able to stand it."

Picking up her head, she set her chin on his chest and looked him square in the eye. "I'll be back as soon as I can, love, promise. Until then, though, I want you to make me a promise, too."

His hazy eyes were warm with adoration and love as he smiled back at her. "Anything, mate."

"Stop watching *The Princess Bride* with the pack's cubs. Only Wesley can get away with 'as you wish'."

She could tell she had absolutely shocked the alpha of the Battletown Pack for a few rare seconds. However, it didn't last long, and Dia ended up scrambling and squealing as she tried to make a break for the bathroom before her mate could retaliate for picking on him. Too bad she only had just put both feet on the floor when Stone scooped her back onto the bed and started tickling her.

His fingers ran up and down her supersensitive ribs until she was begging, "Mercy. Have mercy!" through her squeals of laughter.

The tickling stopped, and she found herself pinned to the bed by Stone, with him lying between her legs again as he smiled down at her.

Damn, she was really going to miss this man while she was gone. Internally, she consoled herself that it was only for a little while. She would be back with the man she loved soon enough.

# *Chapter Four*

***Four hours later…***

Dia stood next to her car, glaring at Stone. "Get out of my way."

Her mate was leaning against her driver's side car door, blocking her from opening it and getting in.

"No."

She had been arguing with the stubborn man for twenty minutes, and she was quickly losing her patience.

"Stone, I love you with all my heart, but if you don't move out of my way and let me go see my family, then I'm going in that house"—she pointed to their home—"and I'm going to get the griddle so I can knock you upside the head with it!"

Stone curled his lip and playfully growled at her.

Dia turned her pointed finger at him. "Don't give me that lip and growl crap, either, mister. You're acting like a big baby right now, and I don't have time for this shit."

A mischievous twinkle lit Stone's eyes as he stepped forward and grabbed the hand with the finger pointing at him. "If I'm a baby, then I get to suck your tits. Let's go; I like this idea."

Dia dug her heels into the ground as Stone started to drag her back toward the house. "Nope, nope, nope!" she yelled as she tugged to try to get her hand back. It was futile because her mate was ten times stronger than her, but he was also paranoid of hurting her since he considered her a fragile human, so he stopped on her third tug.

Turning to face her with an unhappy scowl, Dia didn't give him the chance to speak as she pointed a finger in his direction.

"Just because you're all big and mighty here with the pack doesn't mean you can boss me around and tell me where I can and cannot go."

Slowly, one eyebrow raised to his hairline, silently mocking her. "The fact that I'm alpha means that's exactly what I can do."

She shook her head and folded her arms across her chest. "No, Stone, that's how you treat the pack. That's not how you treat your mate. If you love and respect me at all, you'll try and understand that."

Stone crossed his arms, mimicking her stance. "And if I tell you that I love you so much I just want to protect you?"

Sighing in frustration, Dia closed the distance between them and put her hands on his chest. She knew touch was important to shifters, and it could also be very comforting.

"Just what exactly are you trying to protect me from? My parents? I assure you they would never harm me."

Stone uncrossed his arms, wrapped one around her waist and used his other hand to rub the back of his neck. "I can't explain it, sweetheart, but every instinct I have is screaming not to let you go. I know I'm coming across as a straight up jackass, and I'm sorry. But neither the wolf nor I want to let you go anywhere without us."

It was hard for Dia to be mad when she could see the sincerity in his eyes. Her poor wolf was that worried about her.

Cradling his face in her hands, as she loved to do so often, Dia looked her distressed mate in the eye. "What will make you feel better? Besides staying here with you, because that's not an option."

Stone's frown intensified. "Short of you talking to me the entire drive there, I don't think there's anything that will make me feel better."

Slick wolf. He probably thought Dia wouldn't agree to that because he knew she hated talking on the phone. The ride to her parents' house was going to take almost three hours, so to be on the phone for the entire drive would be pure hell. But she would do it for him.

Without saying another word, Dia sighed dramatically, purposely letting her mate think he had won. Then she pulled out her cell phone and pushed the button to dial Stone's number.

He watched her movements closely, and even though they were standing two inches apart, he pulled his own phone out and answered it. "Yes?" He cocked an eyebrow at her while waiting for a response.

"Agreed," she said to both the phone and her now shocked mate, who was still standing in front of her.

Leaning forward, she kissed Stone on the lips then pulled back to talk into her phone, making her point obvious.

"Now, get the hell out of my way. I'm going to have to plug my phone into the car charger if we're going to talk for three hours."

Stone grudgingly stepped to the side, letting his mate get in her car. Dia started the engine, buckled up, and put the car in drive, all while holding the cell phone to her ear. Then, when she was ready to go, she blew a kiss at Stone and drove off.

Their line was silent as Stone stood there, watching her car drive down the dirt road from their place, and then disappear out of sight. He didn't know what to say, except for "come back," and this trip obviously meant too much to his mate to do that, so he didn't mutter the words.

He walked into the house, closed the front door, and sat in his favorite chair to brood in silence, completely forgetting that he still had his phone at his ear, until Dia snapped, "Well, are you going to say something or what? Because three hours of silence would be ridiculous!"

# *Chapter Five*

*Two weeks later...*

"You're not going to make me talk to you for three hours on the way home, are you?" Dia asked her ornery mate.

"No," Stone snapped through the line.

The man had been unbearable since she had left to visit her parents and take care of her mom after her surgery. Dia had dutifully called three times a day—morning, noon, and night—fulfilling her mate's demands for contact. Had that been good enough for him? Nooooooooooooo.

As much as she loved her wolf, she was starting to consider how nice a wolf skin rug might look as a welcome mat at her hair salon.

"Why are you being so snappy with me, mister? I've done everything you asked me to do since I left!"

"You don't want to know," Stone grumbled back.

"If I didn't want to know, I wouldn't have asked. So again, what's your problem?"

"I'm horny!" her mate roared back. "And if you don't hurry up and get the hell home so I can be inside you, I will track you down and mount you wherever it is I find you. I don't care if it's on the side of the road. So, I suggest you get that sweet ass moving, princess, and come home."

Caught somewhere between amused and annoyed, Dia said, "I told you not to call me princess. I'm not a fucking princess."

When a deep growl came through the phone line, Dia gave in.

"Okay, okay, I'm leaving now, you impatient mutt. I'll call you when I'm an hour away, okay?"

"Good. Love you. Hurry the fuck up." *Click.*

Dia looked at the phone and rolled her eyes. She wasn't sure if she should be excited or scared about going home. From the sound of her mate, he just might fuck her through their mattress.

Wait ... Maybe that wouldn't be so bad.

Dia turned to walk back into her parents' house. She needed to say good-bye. Not to mention, she wanted to check on her mom one last time before she left.

She was only a few steps from the front door when the world exploded right in front of her face.

Literally.

~~~

"Ma'am? Ma'am, can you hear me?" a soft, feminine voice asked.

At least, she thought the voice was trying to be soft. With the way her head hurt, there was a possibility that the person was screaming the words. Every syllable felt like a hammer to her head.

Slowly opening her eyes, she winced at the bright light that blinded her. She tried to pick her hand up to shield her eyes, but she didn't have the strength to do it. It was better just to keep her eyes closed.

"Where am I?" she croaked.

"You're in Vanderbilt University Medical Center."

Trying to think past the pounding in her brain, she asked out loud, but more to herself, "Why in the world am I in the hospital?"

There was a short pause before the voice spoke again. "Do you remember anything that happened?"

Without thought, she went to shake her head no, but that made her groan out in pain. "No," she croaked in answer, instead.

A shadow fell over her eyelids and a soft hand grabbed her own. "Can you open your eyes for me, now please?"

Knowing that the blinding light was blocked for her, she tentatively opened her eyes and immediately saw a brunette in a white uniform leaning over her. She didn't have time to ask who the woman was before her guest spoke first.

"Do you remember your name?"

Her mouth opened to respond, but nothing came out. Her mind was drawing a total blank.

Starting to become more than a little scared, she searched her mind for something, anything, and still came up with nothing. It was a blank slate where she was sure memories should have been. Her eyes watered with tears as she closed her mouth and gently shook her head no.

The woman hovering above her gave her a kind, but sad smile. "Your name is Dia Connor. Do you know how old you are?"

Her name was Dia? She knew she was supposed to be trying to figure out her age, but she was stuck on the name. It was pretty … and different. Surely she should have been able to remember a name like that? That led her to realize something bad must have happened to her.

"Miss," the kind woman called to gain her attention again. "You're zoning out on me. Do you know how old you are?"

Dia searched the recesses of her mind and still found nothing. Even the thought of her name seemed foreign to her. She gently shook her head no again and started to cry.

The woman took her hand off Dia's and, in a nurturing manner, ran her hand over Dia's hair. "Shhh, don't cry. It's going to be okay, Dia. I'm just trying to gauge if your memory is intact."

"What happened to me?" Dia asked her on a frightened croak. "Why am I here? Why can't I remember my own name?" The questions came out in a rush. She couldn't stop herself as a bubble of anxiety started filling her chest so fast she thought her heart might burst from it. "Who are you?" she finally cried out.

The woman was still trying to soothe Dia with soft hushes and comforting touches, but it wasn't really working. Not that she could tell the lady that past the ginormous clog of emotions she had lodged in her throat now.

"My name is Dr. Bennett, and I work here at Vanderbilt. My job is to take care of you and help you heal." She suddenly looked up from Dia to across the room and spoke to someone who was out of Dia's line of sight.

"Nurse, please give her valium. We're going to need her to relax and sleep some more."

"Wait!" Dia shouted, scared at not knowing what was going on. "Before you go, please tell me what happened!"

Dr. Bennett looked back down at Dia with a stoic expression. "Miss Connor, you were involved in an accident. There was a gas explosion, and you just barely missed the worst part of it. You are lucky to have survived the blast."

Out of the corner of her eye, Dia could see the nurse injecting something into her IV line.

Totally dumbfounded at what she had just been told, she squinted at the bright light around her while asking the doctor, "How long have I been here?"

Dr. Bennett bent back over so she could block the light from her eyes again, "You've been in a medically-induced coma for two months, Miss Connor. Now I know you must have lots of questions for me, but I need you to lie back and try to get some more rest, okay? I'll be back to check on you in a couple of hours."

She watched as Dr. Bennett walked away then stood just outside of the room's doorway, writing on what was presumably Dia's chart. The nurse walked out with her and stopped right next to her, quietly bringing the door to a close. Thing was, she didn't close it all the way. There was a small crack, and as fogginess started to impair her thoughts, she could still hear the nurse talking to the doctor.

"It's so tragic what happened to her and her family. And it looks like she doesn't remember a thing. When are you going to tell her that her parents were killed in the explosion?"

Dia's heart clenched so hard in her chest that, for a moment, she wondered if she was having a heart attack. Even though she couldn't place a face to the thought of having a mother and father, it still broke her heart to know that they were now gone. Dia might never remember them again.

Her heart monitor went crazy as her chest started to tighten even more, and the nurse rushed back in to check on Dia. "Miss Connor, are you okay?"

Tears ran silently down her face as she watched the nurse check the machines that had her heart monitor and blood pressure on it. The nurse turned back to her and said, "You're safe here, Miss Connor. I need you to try to calm down. It's not good for the baby for you to be this upset."

The edges of her vision became black, and the haziness she had felt earlier was now stronger than ever. Dia's heart was still pounding away in her chest, but it wasn't enough to keep her awake. Nor was the shock from the nurse's words.

In all honesty, through the frantic thoughts racing through her mind, Dia realized she was probably more lightheaded because she was about to pass out than from the meds they had given her. All because of one little word.

Baby.

And as the black in her vision spread, her chest gasping for air, Dia had one last thought before she passed out. *What baby?*

# *Chapter Six*

"I got the information you wanted … and it's not good."

Stone sat in his dark living room, not needing the light to see the beta of his pack, Caleb, standing across from him, near his front door.

His mood was black with the multiple conflicts going on in his life, and he couldn't help snorting in derision at his beta's words. There wasn't much for Stone to like these days, period.

First, he'd had problems with Sulphur Springs', the visiting pack, delegate. Negotiations for a truce had gone horribly, and the man had left in such a way that Stone was sure that war was about to be on his doorstep. He had sent Caleb to Sulphur Springs to speak directly to the alpha, asking for another meeting, this time with him personally. Surprisingly, the Sulphur Springs' alpha had agreed, and said he would be here in Battletown as soon as he could make it. As soon as he could make it had turned out to be a week and a half later, which meant he had come back to visit the same day that Dia should have been coming home. The problem was, she never did.

That brought him to his next problem. His wolf had been fighting for control from the moment their mate had gone missing. Not that he didn't know where she was now. He did. It had taken him no more than a day to track down her parents' house in Nashville, Tennessee, and find nothing but charred remains. From that point, it had been easy to find out what had happened because it was all over the news. However, the situation had spiraled out of his control from the moment he had stepped foot in the hospital to see her.

The police on site there had not so politely told him that he could not see Dia because he wasn't listed as a known contact for her, nor was he a relative. She was under police supervision until they determined whether the explosion was an accident or intentional.

At the thought that someone might have purposely tried to hurt her, his wolf had snapped, causing him to lose control of his temper. It escalated to the point that he had punched one of the officers in the face when they wouldn't let him see her. Then they had escorted him off the grounds and told him he was banned from coming back.

There he had stood, in another state, unable to see his injured, but thankfully alive mate, and losing his ever-loving mind about it. If that hadn't been bad enough, his beta had called him while he stood just outside of the perimeter of the hospital grounds and delivered another blow.

In Stone's haste to find his mate, he had dismissed the visiting Sulphur Springs alpha, and in doing so, insulted him greatly. Not that he gave two fucks about it when it came down to trying to get to his injured mate, which was exactly what he had told Caleb. All of his concentration had been on finding out if his mate was okay.

Fucking Caleb had thrown the truth back in his face. Stone needed to care. Otherwise, he might inadvertently start a pack war with the very pack he had been trying to make an ally. It was at that moment that the police officer he had punched pulled up in his patrol car and told him to leave or he would arrest him for assault after all.

Stone had no choice but to leave, with only a promise to himself, and his raging wolf, that he would come back soon and find a way in to see Dia. Only, when he had checked into a hotel, shit seemed to spiral out of control again. He had twenty-four hours to come back, meet with the visiting alpha, and apologize, or it would be full-out war between Stone's Battletown Pack and their closest non-human neighbors, the Sulphur Springs Pack.

Stone had been left with an unconceivable decision to make: Stay there in Tennessee for his injured mate, or go back to Kentucky and make peace for his pack's sake.

Two months later, he still fucking hated himself for leaving his mate that day. Although he had sent three of his most trusted pack members to search over the hospital for any signs of her, and to protect her if need be, it wasn't the same. He should have been there with Dia, and not here in Kentucky dealing with this bullshit, even if he had discovered that it was for her best interests that he had left her.

A week after her parents' house exploded, Stone had accomplished two very important things. First, he had made amends with the Sulphur Springs alpha and had secured that alliance. Then the three pack members watching over Dia's hospital reported back with the unthinkable. The Connor's house explosion had been no accident. Someone had purposely set that gas leak so that it would cause an explosion. It was all over the local news there in Tennessee and the human investigators were trying to figure out who had done it. That made Stone wonder: who exactly was the perpetrator trying to kill? Dia's parents, or Dia herself?

No matter the answer, Stone had to find out who had done this so he could make sure his mate was safe, and so he could get her justice for losing her parents. That was something Caleb had been helping him with for almost two months now. The problem was, they were having a hard time figuring out who had started the gas leak and why.

Now Caleb stood in his living room with an answer, and the hair standing up on the back of Caleb's neck told him Stone wasn't going to like it.

"What is it?" Stone asked with no preamble.

His beta crossed his arms over his chest and shifted his weight from one foot to the other. He was on edge, and had been since they had discovered the attempt made on Dia's life.

"I don't know who exactly, Stone. I've only uncovered why Dia's parents' house exploded."

A snarl escaped Stone, and he had to reel his wolf back in. He gripped the arms of his chair tight, using all his willpower to keep the powerful beast at bay, when he really wanted to let him loose for bloodshed.

"WHY THEN?" he snarled out in anger.

Caleb uncrossed his arms and ran a hand through his hair. The need to fidget told Stone that his beta was probably battling his own wolf for control, too.

"I was on patrol and behind Old Man Grayson's barn when I heard two feminine voices. They didn't realize I was there because I was downwind. They were talking about the attempt on Dia's life failing and how someone was going to have to finish the job."

"Just to be clear, they said her name?"

Caleb shook his head slowly, then said, "They said 'the alpha's human bitch.' That's how I know they were talking about Dia."

"Did you kill them?" Stone snarled.

When Caleb shook his head no, Stone lost all control. His wolf's anger snapped, and the next thing he knew, Stone was across the room, pinning Caleb to a wall by his throat.

"WHY DIDN'T YOU KILL THEM?" he roared at his beta.

Wheezing for air, Caleb choked out, "Because they heard me coming and disappeared."

Letting go of Caleb, Stone stepped back and tried to regain his composure. "What do you mean, they disappeared?"

His beta was rubbing his throat, trying to soothe the spot where Stone had grabbed him. His voice was still rough when he answered, "I fucked up. Accidentally stepped on a twig that snapped under my paw. They must have heard it, because the next thing I heard was whispered voices and then nothing. By the time I ran around to the other side of the barn, they were gone."

Running his hands through his hair, Stone growled, "Why didn't you follow them?"

His beta stilled unnaturally, and then slowly leaned closer to Stone to whisper, "There was nothing to follow. No visible tracks and no scent. The best I can figure is they were standing in the small stream that runs beside the barn to cover their tracks. What I can't explain is how they left no scent at all."

"That's impossible."

Caleb nodded. "I know. Even though they could have been standing in the water, it still wouldn't have taken much for the water to bring their scent to the area. Nobody ever escapes without leaving some sort of scent trail. What I want to know, man, is how the hell they did it. Because I'm telling you, Stone, I know what I heard. Those voices were *there*. So, why weren't they? Or, at least the faintest trace of them?"

Taking numb steps backward, Stone had frantic thoughts whirling through his mind. Disbelief was one of them. How could someone disappear and not leave a scent track? Hunters used other smells to cover their scents, but that wasn't what Caleb had found—or not found, for that matter. His beta hadn't been able to find anything at all. Which seemed impossible.

*Unless they have a witch.*

"Holy fuck, we have a witch on our hands," Stone whispered in shock.

Caleb's face morphed into one of enraged fury. He hated magic, to the point he was prejudice against it. He had his reasons for it, though. A witch had killed his parents in a spell gone wrong.

Balling his fists up by his sides, Caleb let out an angry growl, his lip curling in distaste. "I'll kill any witch I come across. I swear this to you, Alpha."

Some distant part of Stone's mind heard what his beta was saying, but he was still too much in shock to say anything back. Who would bring a witch onto their lands and why?

His wolf snarled in his head, *To kill our mate.*

All this time, Stone had been trying to figure out why some human would blow up his mate's parents' house. Now he knew humans weren't the ones to blame. There was at least one witch involved, and a conversation held on his pack lands told him the only other thing he needed to know just then. Someone in his pack wanted his mate dead. Now he just had to figure out who and why. Until then …

Stone pulled out his cell phone and dialed one of the wolves who was watching over his mate's hospital.

"Alpha," the other wolf answered with no preamble.

His pack treated him with the utmost respect at all times and seemed to be happy under his reign. Well, at least he thought they had. Now he had to wonder if he really had some unhappy anarchists in his pack who were trying to bring him down through his mate.

He was at least sure that the three wolves he had sent to watch over Dia—Brandt, James, and Scotty—were loyal to a fault. There was no other wolf he trusted more than those three, besides Caleb.

"Someone is trying to kill my mate. Be aware of everything around you and be careful. I'll also need you three to try harder in finding her inside the hospital and keeping an eye on her there. Nothing is to happen to her, you understand?"

"Yes, Alpha," Brandt replied.

"Good. Call me once you have an update about her. I want to know how she's doing." Stone hung the phone up and collapsed back into his chair. Gripping the arms, he felt the entire world fall away as both his human and wolf side focused on one single task.

Find and kill whoever it was who had harmed his mate.

# *Chapter Seven*

Dia gradually came to and opened eyelids that felt like they had hundred-pound weights holding them closed. Dim lighting let her slowly focus on a window with nothing but clear blue sky on the other side of it. Haltingly, she took in the room around her and remembered where she was: the hospital. Flashes of a memory of waking up here before started to play in her mind.

*A doctor telling her she had been in an accident.*

Besides having a splitting headache, she didn't feel sore, so what kind of accident had she been in?

*Overhearing the nurse say something to the doctor about her parents being killed in an explosion.*

Pain and confusion swamped her emotions. Her parents were dead? She didn't even remember having parents, but that didn't stop her chest from hurting at the knowledge that they were dead and she would never meet them or get to know them. It was bad enough that she didn't know who she was, but now that she knew her parents were dead, there was a chance there would be nobody alive to tell her these things. What if she had no other family?

A fast beeping from one of the monitors she was hooked up to started to speed up, so Dia looked over at the machines. It wasn't her heart monitor, she could easily see that number. It was a high number, but there seemed to be no sound to it at the moment. She kept looking until she found another monitor with a second heartbeat, and that was when the last of her flashbacks hit her like a ton of bricks.

*You're safe here, Miss Connor. I need you to try to calm down. It's not good for the baby for you to be this upset.*

Holy Moses on the mountain, was she freaking pregnant?

The shock of that possibility immobilized her. Dia didn't know what to think or what to say. Wait, who was she going to say something to, anyway? Her baby? It wasn't like she knew anyone else right now. Hell, the only reason she knew her name was because the doctor had told her what it was. That made the shock of a pregnancy all the more unsettling because she had no idea who the father was.

Looking down at her waist, she was really concerned not to see an obvious baby belly bulge there. She had a slightly rounded tummy, but that was more of her body shape than a baby bump, she thought. It was obvious from looking down at her ample chest and hips that she had a curvy figure. So if she was pregnant, she must not be very far along, right?

Just then, a woman in a blue uniform came through her door. She was pushing a cart with a food tray on it. "Oh, good, you're awake in time for lunch."

Dia stared at the cheerful woman, not knowing what to say. Not that the nurse seemed to mind. The woman just pushed her cart up next to Dia's bed, then used the remote control for the bed to prop Dia up into a sitting position. Once she had that done, she slid a table over Dia's lap then put a tray of food right in front of her. It was at that moment that her stomach decided to let out a loud groan of hunger, causing the nurse to laugh and her cheeks to warm in embarrassment.

The nurse was chattering away as she got Dia set up with food, utensils, and a drink. Talking about the beautiful weather, she said something that Dia's brain latched on to, as if it should be important.

"It's a shame they had to cut your hair off, honey. I got to see it as they were wheeling you back to the ER, and it was gorgeous."

Dia reached up with both hands and found short, prickly strands covering her head.

*Buzz cut*, her mind whispered to her.

Why in the world would she know what sort of haircut this was? Why would that be so important to her for Dia to actually remember it?

Looking at the nurse, she asked, "How long was my hair?"

The nurse gave her a sad look. "Oh, honey, your hair was glorious. Nice and long, past your shoulders. Good natural wave to it. I was downright jealous over that head of hair. But it couldn't be helped. You hit your head, and there was swelling on the brain. They had to shave it all off to run their tests and see if you needed surgery. You had electrodes attached to your poor little head for over two weeks. At least your hair is starting to grow back now. Well, you eat up now, sugar. Need you to feed that baby growing inside of you."

A strangled noise came from the doorway, making Dia and the nurse both look in that direction, but they didn't see anyone there.

Shrugging her shoulders, the nurse wished Dia good-bye and pushed her cart out of the room, leaving Dia alone again with nothing but her lunch, her scrambled thoughts, and her pitifully short hair.

She picked at the food on her tray, not feeling very hungry. A small grumble in her stomach called her a liar and reminded Dia that she was eating for more than herself now, so she forced herself to take a bite of the meatloaf on her plate. She had just finished that portion of her lunch when there was a knock on her hospital room door.

Dr. Bennett was back.

"Hello, Dia, how are you feeling today?"

Dia shrugged. "Okay, I guess. Still very confused about what's going on more than anything."

The doctor gave her a sad smile. "I would say that's perfectly normal in your circumstance, but that's also why I'm here today—to answer any questions you might have."

Dia chewed on her bottom lip nervously, wondering what she should ask first. There were some things she didn't want to talk about too much, like the loss of the parents she couldn't even remember.

"I remember overhearing that my parents are dead. Is that true?"

Dr. Bennett gave her a small nod. "Yes, unfortunately there was a gas leak at their house and it ignited. You were outside the house, and that's why you're still alive today."

Fresh grief tore through her soul, but it was a necessary pain. Dia had to know what was going on if she was going to somehow take control back of her life.

With a choked voice, Dia asked, "What exactly happened to me?"

The doctor flipped a chart open in front of her and started to read. "The blast from the explosion sent you flying for several feet, and when you landed, you hit your head on the curb of the road. The hit to the head was significant enough to cause a small brain bleed that luckily stopped on its own, but also caused a substantial amount of swelling. We put you in a medically-induced coma while treating the swelling, and it took us two months to get it under control because of the pregnancy."

"So, I am pregnant?" Dia asked with a breathless hitch in her voice.

The doctor nodded again. "Indeed, you are. From the ultrasound we gave you, we have you at approximately two and a half months along. Now it's my turn for a question: do you happen to remember anything?"

Dia shook her head. If she tried hard to look into the recesses of her brain, all she saw was a black blank slate of nothingness.

"Nothing. Will my memories ever come back?"

The doctor gave her an encouraging grin. "I think they will. You see, when your swelling brain tissue pressed against your skull, it caused some impairment, such as memory loss. It can also cause mood swings or erratic behavior. Even though you're awake now, the memory loss and confusion is still there. However, I think you will get at least some of your memory back with time. It's going to come down to having a whole lot of faith and patience."

It wasn't the best news, but it was at least something to look forward to. Dia wished with every fiber of her being that she would get her memory back.

Dr. Bennett seemed ready to leave, though Dia still had one last question for her.

"Doctor, before you go, has no one come to see me? I understand my parents are dead, but do I have no other family? Or perhaps the father of the baby? Maybe I came into the ER with a wedding ring on?"

Dr. Bennett's face lost all of her sparkle and a sad look crossed her face. "I'm sorry, my dear. You had no jewelry on you when you were brought in. We're searching to see if you have any extended family, but so far, we've found none. And no one has been by to see you."

The aura in the room became sad and awkward. More than anything, Dia just wanted to be left alone now.

As if the doctor could read her mind, she told Dia good-bye and said she would be back to check on her again before her rounds were done that day.

There she was, left alone again, with nothing but mashed potatoes and a strawberry jello that she no longer had any desire to eat. Looking at the blue sky out of her hospital room window, Dia wondered sadly if there was anyone left in the world who cared for her at all.

# *Chapter Eight*

"We need a trap."

Caleb's words rang through the silence of Stone's house.

It was hard to think about what needed to be done when he was waiting to hear back from the men he had stationed in Nashville to guard Dia. Instead of hearing about his mate, though, Stone was sitting here with his beta, trying to come up with a plan to catch the people responsible for almost killing Dia.

"What are you thinking?" he asked Caleb.

His beta clenched his hands together where they rested on the tops of his legs. "You're not going to like this, but I think the fastest way to lure them out is to use Dia as bait."

"Not happening," Stone shut his beta down right away.

Holding his hands up in a surrender gesture, Caleb kept trying. "Just hear me out. We announce to the pack that Dia is okay and coming home. Then we keep her surrounded at all times on the way home. We put wolves we trust hidden out of sight around your house, and when we get her here to your place, we make a big pretense of leaving her alone for a little while so you can get some pack business done. I bet whoever it is will try to get to her then. We can take them out here."

"What if they don't come right away? We put her in danger until they do make an attempt? And how do we keep her protected for that long? I think your plan has more holes than swiss cheese. It's been two months since I've seen my mate, and I sure as fuck don't want to put her in danger the moment I finally get her back."

Saying out loud how long he had been away from his mate was hard. Thinking of how frightened she must be was even harder. What worried him the most was that she had not tried to call him in the past two months. Was it because she was unconscious and couldn't? This was why his men needed to hurry up and give him a fucking update.

As if his men knew he was thinking about them and Dia, Stone's cell phone rang.

Putting his hand up to halt Caleb from anymore discussion, he looked at the number on the screen then picked up the phone.

"Update?"

Brandt was the one to answer him. "I made it into the hospital, found her floor and room in the hospital's system when a nurse's back was turned at the main desk. Went up to scope out her room and could hear her talking with the nurse. She's awake and lucid, but I overheard a nurse on her floor say she's lost all her memory."

It felt like the floor dropped out from beneath Stone. "How bad is her memory loss?"

"From what I overheard, she remembers nothing and no one. Didn't even remember her own name when she woke up."

"Fuck!" Stone roared, lifting his arm, ready to throw his phone against the wall. What Brandt said next stopped him from doing it, though.

"There's more."

Taking a deep breath, Stone put the phone back to his ear and prayed the "more" was good news. "Yes?"

"She's pregnant."

Stone would have never thought it possible, but at hearing that news, his wolf went ballistic. Their mate was pregnant with their cub, and he was nowhere near her to protect her. The logical side of his brain reminded him that was a good thing. Someone was out to kill Dia because of him. However, the primal, animalistic part of him was raging to run to his mate and protect her.

Waring emotions ran through him until he just wanted to kick Caleb out of his place so he could be left alone to process everything. What happiness and joy he felt at the knowledge that he was going to have a baby with the woman he loved was quickly overshadowed by the reality of their situation. Now he had two people to protect instead of one. Dia was carrying his son or daughter, and there wasn't a damn thing in this world that he would ever let touch his child.

Turning his attention back to Brandt, he ordered, "Stay as close to her as you can without being noticed. In fact, is there a waiting room near her room?"

"There's a waiting room just down the hall from her. What do you want us to do?"

"The three of you rotate in shifts, staying in the waiting room. Close enough that you can hear what's going on without tipping anyone off that you're not supposed to be there. Call me anytime you learn something new. Caleb and I will continue to work on things from our end. If anyone from the pack calls you, tell them I sent you on a business trip."

Brandt sounded a little confused when he asked, "Are we not telling the pack that Dia is hurt?"

Looking straight into Caleb's eyes, he made sure the man was paying attention to his conversation so he only had to say this once. "No, we're going to tell the pack that Dia died from complications. As far as the pack is concerned, she's dead to them. Understood?"

"Yes sir," Brandt answered, and then Stone hung up the phone.

Caleb, however, looked less understanding and more confused than anything. "Why are we going to tell the pack that Dia died?"

Stone pursed his lips together and narrowed his eyes. "You heard what Brandt said. Dia is pregnant with my cub. There's no way in hell I'm letting you talk me into using her as bait now. No, we'll figure something else out and leave my mate and child safe in Nashville."

"Have any ideas how you want to lure out her would-be killers, then?" Caleb asked.

Shaking his head, Stone told him the truth. "Not a fucking clue. Put your thinking cap on because I want this mystery solved as soon as possible. Until we figure out a way to draw them out, we have a pack to go tell that their alpha's mate is dead. Let's go get this shit over with."

# *Chapter Nine*

***One week later…***

"It's almost time for you to leave."

Dia clenched her hands together over her stomach, thinking about the baby that lay just beneath them. Giving voice to her worries, she asked the nurse, who had been so kind to her this past week, "Where will I go? I don't know anyone or anything. I don't know if I have any extended family or friends. I don't even know if I have a place of my own, or if I was staying with my parents in the house that exploded! And, if all of that isn't bad enough, I'm pregnant and don't even know how I got that way or who the baby's father is!" She was almost sobbing by the time she finished her sentence.

The nurse held her hands up in a silent request for her to stop. "Hold on, honey. Just calm down. That's what I'm here to talk to you about. There's a place a little ways from here that takes in expecting mothers who have no place to live. I've called them, and they said you could come stay with them."

"Yeah, but for how long?" Dia asked desperately. "How long will they let me stay? I may never get my memories back."

The nurse sat down on the side of her bed and patted her hand. "Don't worry about everything at once, honey. You need to take things one step at a time. Right now, the best thing you can do for you, your baby, and your memory is get back to living life. What's not good for you is to stress too much."

Letting her head fall back on her pillow, Dia couldn't help the tears that started running down her face. How could she not stress right now? She was a woman who was almost three months pregnant, with no home and no money. That was a tough situation to bring a baby into.

She felt another soft pat to her hand and looked back at the nurse.

"It's gonna be all right. I've been on the phone with some churches and charities. The other nurses and I are gonna do everything we can to help you and the baby. Until then, honey, you have to keep the hope alive. Your memories can return, and while that won't solve everything, it's still something to look forward to. Until then, look forward to that precious bundle you're carrying. In a little over a month, you'll be able to find out if you're having a boy or a girl. Isn't that something to look forward to?"

Dia glanced down at her belly, which was now starting to show a small baby bump. It was more like a pooch, but there was no doubt in her mind that it was her baby under that small mound. She thought about finding out the baby's sex and found the thought bittersweet. That was probably something she should be doing with the baby's father, if she only knew who he was. The nurse was right about one thing, though. She needed to try to stay positive for the baby's sake. It was important for her to take care of herself while she had the proverbial bun in the oven.

The nurse's voice brought Dia out of her musings. "Do you want a girl or a boy, honey?"

Dia gave her the only answer she could think of. "It doesn't matter to me. I just want a family, and this baby is going to give me that."

# *Chapter Ten*

"How are you doing, Alpha?"

Stone was standing at the fake memorial service for his mate, hoping that whoever had tried to kill her was in this room. He had been without her for far too long, and he was more than ready to figure out this mystery so he could bring Dia home. Even though his patience was non-existent, and his wolf was raging inside of him, he somehow managed to play the part of a grieving widower to the little old lady standing before him.

He let some of his agitation show because that was how a wolf who had recently lost their mate would act. A twitch of his eye, the tightening of his hands, and a low rumbling growl in his chest. Then Stone reeled it all back in so he didn't give in to the urge to bite his packmate's head off.

"It's very kind of you to ask, Mrs. Jones, but to be honest, I'm not doing well. I'd rather have Dia here with me more than anything." The words he spoke were true, even if no one in this room beyond Caleb knew that his mate was actually alive in Nashville. Everyone would assume he meant he would rather have his dead mate back. It was a simple trick of the words so that no one could discern he was lying.

The hunched over, ninety-year-old woman clucked her tongue at him. "Now, now. Wouldn't do for the alpha to give up on us. Perk up, my boy; it'll be okay. I lost my Wilbur fifty years ago, and I'm still chugging along. You will, too."

Utterly shocked at her words, Stone didn't have a chance to respond to her callous statement before she moved away. He watched her toddle over to her great-granddaughter, Danielle, who stood next to the building's door, fidgeting from foot to foot. Her hands were clenched in front of her and nervousness rolled off her in waves.

Stone felt someone stop next to him and knew it was his beta by the scent, so he muttered under his breath where only Caleb could hear, "Someone looks nervous."

"Or guilty," Caleb murmured back.

Looking back at his beta, he asked almost hopefully, "Have you had a chance to hear her speak?"

Caleb shook his head. "Danielle hasn't uttered a word all afternoon. I would say that is odd, unless she's afraid I'll recognize her voice from that day behind the barn."

"Exactly," Stone muttered. "Keep her under surveillance, but make sure to stay hidden. The minute you hear her speak, I want to know if she was one of the two voices you heard. Otherwise, this whole sham today was a waste of time."

"Have faith, my friend. We'll get whoever it is that did this."

With that, Caleb moved to mingle back in the crowd as Danielle and Mrs. Jones left the building. His beta couldn't follow them just yet. He needed to be here, on the off chance that their would-be killer was still in the room. Although, the more Stone watched the spot that Mrs. Jones and her great-granddaughter had just left, the more he became certain that the conspirators against his mate had just left the room.

~~~

Several hours later, Stone sat in his chair, staring into nothing, with his lights on, giving the pack the pretense he was at home, mourning again. Really what he was doing was waiting. Waiting on his beta to call him with news.

Caleb was currently staking out Danielle's house.

The two men had stayed until they sweet talked the last guest to leave the memorial so the poor alpha could go home. The reason that they had stayed after

Mrs. Jones and Danielle had left had been a bust. Out of everyone who had come, which had been the entire Battletown Pack, none of them had matched one of the voices that Caleb had heard that day behind the barn. Danielle Jones had been the only pack-member who Caleb had not heard speak. It seemed as though, slowly, the evidence was starting to pile up against her, which made Stone wonder: Had the day Dia had almost been hit by Mrs. Jones SUV been an accident after all?

He could have sworn it had been the old woman driving that day, but perhaps it had been Danielle instead. If things had gone differently, he could have very well lost Dia before he had ever had her. The thought turned his blood ice cold and made his stomach drop.

Sitting here, waiting, was driving him insane, but there was nothing else he could do right now. The plan was in motion, his beta was in place, and now all they needed was for Danielle Jones to open her mouth and say something.

An hour later, Stone got the phone call he had been impatiently waiting for.

Picking it up, he asked Caleb the only question that mattered. "Is it her?"

"Yes."

Triumph and rage both surged through him at the single word. He finally had one of the two people who had conspired to kill his mate. Now they just had to grab Danielle and find out who else was involved.

"I'll be there in just a minute. Wait for me. If she tries to leave the house, grab her."

Finally, after months of trying to find out who had attacked his mate, he was going to have justice.

Stone hung up the phone, jumped out of his chair, and raced out of his house and to his truck. Throwing himself into it, he started the engine and slammed his foot on the gas pedal. Tires screeched, the motor roared, and he catapulted forward down his driveway. Danielle and her great-grandmother only lived minutes from him, but he couldn't get there fast enough.

He made the five-minute drive in two and a half minutes, slamming on his brakes and sliding to a stop on the side of the road where he saw Caleb waiting for him. Throwing the car in park, he then jumped out of his truck, not even bothering to close the door, and rounded the hood, heading straight for old lady Jones's house.

He didn't bother knocking on the door. As alpha, he took his pack-given right to kick that bitch in. In fact, he kicked the door so hard, he ripped the top half off its hinges.

Caleb was right on his heels as Stone stormed into the house with an enraged roar.

Danielle came into view, running in to see what had happened to her front door. She took one look at Stone, his angry countenance, and how fast he was approaching her, then tried to flee. She had a right to be scared. It didn't matter if she was a female, Stone didn't plan to spare her any more than she had planned to spare his mate.

What caught the alpha totally off guard, though, was Danielle screaming for her great-grandmother.

"They're here! Run, Grandma Jones! They're here for us!"

Stone and Caleb were hot on Danielle's heels, chasing her through the house, within grabbing reach of her, when little old woman Jones stepped out from behind the kitchen door and threw something in his face.

Between one second and the next, Stone's legs wouldn't work. He tried to catch himself as he started to fall, but his hands and arms wouldn't work, either. That was why he went crashing to the ground, completely immobile within seconds.

From the floor, Stone watched as Caleb roared while batting the old woman's hands down. Grabbing her from behind, he secured Mrs. Jones's hands behind her back as her granddaughter escaped out the back door.

The old woman began to mutter strange rhymes before Caleb wrapped his hand around her mouth to stop her.

Magic.

The old bitty had found herself some magic.

It was too much. His wolf didn't leave things to chance. Someone using magic when they weren't born to ... Well, that meant things could easily get out of control.

Which seemed to be the case here.

Caleb let out a yelp as old lady Jones bit his hand.

Stone was beginning to get movement back just in the nick of time to shove a dishtowel from the kitchen into the woman's mouth.

After glaring at Mrs. Jones, Caleb cocked an eyebrow at him.

"At the risk of getting my ass beat, I have to say it. I can't believe you let a ninety-year-old lady take you out, boss."

Irritated that his beta was right, Stone countered, "She didn't take me out; she just caught me by surprise. Now stop trying to piss me off and make sure she's securely tied up."

Caleb glared at Mrs. Jones as he took his leather belt off while holding the old woman still with his other hand. "I think she's got a few more surprises for us. Like who the hell she's getting magic from." Done talking, Caleb tied Mrs. Jones's feet to the chair that Stone had put in front of him, then looked back. "Think we can track Danielle down?"

Stone shook his head. "I might have been unable to move, but my hearing worked just fine. She got in a car and took off. We'll never catch up to her tonight. Call our enforcers and tell them to be on the lookout for her. While you do that, I'm going to call Miriam. It's time Mrs. Jones faced the pack's female alpha."

Silence fell around them.

Stone didn't understand why Caleb wasn't on his phone yet, so he looked at the man for answers. What he found was a strange, perplexed look on his beta's face.

"What?"

Caleb looked down at the ground, his Adam's apple bobbing as he took a nervous swallow.

Not having the patience for this sort of shit, Stone snapped, "Just spit it out."

His beta winced, then picked up his head and told Stone, "Boss, don't call your mom by her first name. It's just weird."

Caleb didn't even flinch when his alpha lost control and roared in his face.

# *Chapter Eleven*

"Now, sugar, I don't know who the baby's daddy is, but I bet your baby comes out with your gorgeous hair."

The lunch nurse who was always so nice to her was back visiting Dia later that evening. The sky was a dark blue, on its way to a nighttime black.

Dia was grateful for the woman's visit since she wasn't tired yet. The older African-American woman, whose name she learned was Angela, sat in a chair next to her bed and smiled her sunny smile that Dia found infectious.

"Why do you think that?" Dia asked the nurse softly.

The woman's smile somehow got even brighter as she said, "No one with hair as pretty as yours could not pass that on to their baby. Just you watch, honey. That little blessing in your belly is going to come out with your strawberry blonde locks. And if it's a girl … Whoo-wee! You better get a shotgun ready, because the boys will come from all over."

She couldn't help laughing at Angela's enthusiasm. It felt good to laugh. She hadn't had much reason to do that since she had woken up.

Angela patted her hand to get her attention. "Tomorrow, you're going to be discharged, and I'm going to take you to the Fresh Start Women's Center. You ready to get your life going again, sugar?"

Dia shrugged, uncertain. Using her free hand to rub over her belly, she thought about being out in the world again. She might miss Angela's visits, and the friendly staff here, but she wouldn't miss being made to rest in the hospital.

Turning back toward Angela, she finally nodded. "I'm ready. I appreciate everything you all have done for me, but I don't want to be here anymore. I want to go out and figure how I'm going to take care of me and my baby."

Angela gave her another soft pat on the hand. "I'm so happy to hear you say that, honey. Now get some rest. Tomorrow, you'll start your journey, and I've got a feeling it's going to lead you exactly where you're meant to go.

As she watched the nurse leave, Dia prayed the woman was right and that she would end up where she was meant to be.

*I just want to find my home.*

# *Chapter Twelve*

He watched her walk through the door, head back, shoulders squared, and utterly confident. It wasn't a surprise to see Miriam that way. Stone had seen his mother act that way for as long as he could remember. She was the alpha female of their pack, just as his father had been the alpha male. When Stone's father had passed away, Stone had assumed that role. Not just because he was his father's only child, but because the entire pack knew he was the strongest, most cunning, and definitely the most lethal out of all of them.

When it came to women, though? Not his department.

Sure, he could pass judgement on a female of his pack, but this was more. They needed to find out how old Mrs. Jones had come into her magic, and who else, other than her great-granddaughter, she was working with.

Stone watched as Caleb bowed his head in deference to his mother, but the old woman didn't. It was a snub that he knew would not go unpunished by his mother, which was very bad for Mrs. Jones, because Miriam had been mourning the loss of Dia since the day Stone had told the pack she had died.

His mother had loved Dia from the first moment she had met her, and had treated her as a daughter right away. Even though he knew he could trust her, he hadn't even told his own mother that his mate was still very much alive. And after losing her own mate five years ago, Miriam had taken the loss of Stone's mate harder than anyone else in the pack. Now she was looking for vengeance on Dia's behalf.

"Tell me, Patty; why would you do anything to harm your alpha?"

Mrs. Jones turned her head away.

His mother spoke again. "Tell me why you tried to hurt my son."

The little old lady spat in Stone's direction. "He's no alpha to me! The moment he mated that human whore, he stopped being my alpha. I tried to stop it, too! That day in the street in front of the human whore's shop, I almost killed her then. It would have saved him from the human's clutches! He just had to go and save her, though. I knew then they would probably mate, and if he did, I decided he was a lost cause. But I'll be damned if I follow a man who fornicates with human filth. Imagine if they had a child together! Blasphemy. It would be an utter abomination. We need to keep our shifter lines pure, and the human tart was only going to corrupt him."

Miriam stepped in front of Mrs. Jones's chair and bent down until she was nose to nose with the bitter woman. "That human was my daughter, and whether you liked it or not, your alpha's mate. You know what the sentence is for someone who makes an attempt on an alpha or his mate? Death. Tell me now, Patty, why you attacked my son tonight, and what you had to do with the attack on his mate, and I'll forgo the death sentence."

"I'd rather you kill me, you human-loving bitch." Mrs. Jones sniffed in annoyance, as if none of them were worth her time.

That was a serious mistake on her part.

His mother grabbed the arms of the chair and stared at the old woman until Mrs. Jones looked away, a reminder of who was alpha here and who was not. Stone knew Miriam wouldn't torture the woman because of her old age. His mother might be lethal, but she drew certain lines in the sand and refused to cross them. It would be interesting to see how she chose to handle this problem. It didn't take long for him to find out.

Using one hand to grab Mrs. Jones by her wrinkly face, Miriam growled and flashed her fangs. "You'll tell me what I want to know, or I'll end you, old woman. I don't need a pack hearing to be your judge, jury, and executioner tonight."

"I already told you to kill me, then."

Miriam shook her head. "That's not all I'll do. You'll tell me how you came to obtain the magic, and who else was involved in this scheme besides your great-granddaughter, or I'll exile your whole line after I kill Danielle in front of them."

Mrs. Jones sucked in a sharp breath, as if she couldn't believe Miriam would carry through on her threat. It was by far the harshest sentence in pack history.

"Think of it, Patty," his mother whispered. "Think of how I'll snap Danielle's neck in front of every person who's remotely related to you before I banish them from our pack. They'll have no place to go, no way to eat, and nowhere to call home, all thanks to you. And the best part? I have better plans for you now. See, for you, instead of killing you, I'll leave you alive so that you have to leave with them. Eventually, one of them will get so angry at you for what you've done that they'll kill you themselves. Is that how you want to end? By the hands of your own kin? Despised and left to rot in the middle of nowhere?"

Mrs. Jones struggled to pull her face out of his mother's grip, but failed. It took her a few minutes to stop fighting to get free, but eventually, the reality of not only her situation, but that of her children's and grandchildren's, must have sunk in as she started to cry silent tears.

"I made Danielle do it. It's not the child's fault; it's all mine," Mrs. Jones sobbed.

"Where did you get the magic, Patty?"

Mrs. Jones opened her mouth to answer, but no words came out. They watched her get frustrated as she did this several times, before Stone figured out what was going on.

"She's been spelled not to speak the name."

The old woman nodded furiously, agreeing with him, as Caleb suggested, "Should we untie her hands to let her write it down?"

Mrs. Jones nodded again as the beta looked at his two alphas for the final answer.

Stone was ready to tell him yes, when his mother put a hand to Patty's shoulder and said, "Not without some ground rules first." Leaning back down to look Mrs. Jones directly in the eye, she said, "If you make one suspicious move to cast any more magic, I will personally guarantee the torture of Danielle for a long, long time before I finally kill her. You understand me, old woman? Your actions can mean a great deal of pain to your own kin."

Mrs. Jones nodded warily this time, and then Miriam gave Caleb the signal to untie her hands.

Looking around, Stone saw a notebook and pen on an end table next to the sofa and walked over to pick it up. When he turned back around, Mrs. Jones was rubbing her red, raw wrists and watching Stone with pure hatred. He didn't give her the satisfaction of a reaction, just handed the notebook and pen to their captive and gruffly ordered, "Write it down now."

*Sulphur Springs Pack*

*Alpha's daughter is a witch.*

*She blew house up.*

"How in the fuck is a shifter also a witch?" Caleb bellowed angrily.

Mrs. Jones sat there with a shit-eating grin on her face, as if she knew the answer and would never tell. The old bitch probably did know.

The sting of betrayal ran through Stone again as he looked at those words and wondered if the alpha he had spoken to during negotiations had known what his daughter was doing. It would mean war if he had. Stone would never let something like this go. That witch had been the one to kill his mate's parents, and very nearly his mate and cub, too.

None of them had time to say a word before, faster than any ninety-year-old woman had a right to move, Mrs. Jones took that pen and shoved it into her own neck.

No one had seen it coming, and truly, even if Mrs. Jones hadn't already been facing a death sentence, they wouldn't have been able to help her, anyway.

The spurting from the hole in her neck let them know that she had hit her carotid artery and would bleed out in minutes.

The old woman had decided to go out on her terms rather than theirs.

As much as Stone hated her, he understood that sentiment. He wouldn't want anyone controlling his future or death, either.

Stone, his mother, and Caleb stepped away as Mrs. Jones slumped in her chair, letting her life literally drain away. Red covered the old woman's neck and, little by little, the spurting slowed down until it was just leaking in a small, steady flow. Her eyelids flickered a few times before they closed and didn't reopen again.

The three of them stood there, watching as one problem passed away, leaving them with two more: the witch in Sulphur Springs and Danielle. Now the question was: Which problem should he go after first?

His mother grabbed his arm and pulled, indicating he should leave.

"Caleb and I will deal with this. You go track down Danielle."

Stopping her on the house's doorstep, Stone said, "Wait, Mom, there's something I need to tell you."

Stone knew he was doing the right thing by telling her his secret when his mother looked at him with sad eyes.

Pulling her closer so he could whisper in his mother's ear, Stone told her the truth, "Dia survived the blast. She's alive in a Tennessee hospital." Pulling back, he looked for his mother's reaction and found tears and a shocked smile on her face.

"Truly?" she whispered, almost as if she was afraid to hope.

He nodded then leaned in and whispered again, "And she's pregnant."

His mother grabbed at his shirt and tugged him into a hug as she sobbed for joy. They stayed that way for several minutes. Anyone who would have seen them would never know that the alpha female was crying tears of joy, instead of tears of loss. It was their secret now, until he could bring his mate home and explain what had happened to the pack.

Eventually, his mother pushed out of his embrace and wiped the tears from her face. "Go. Find Danielle so we can finish this. We're overdue for some peace and good news in this pack."

It was easy to understand what his mother wasn't saying, never knowing if there were other ears listening. *Hurry up and finish so I can be a grandma.*

Turning away, Stone somehow managed to hide the smile that threatened to break out across his face as he headed toward his truck. He was mentally going through the possibilities of where Danielle might have gone when his cell phone rang. It was the Sulphur Springs' alpha's phone number.

Putting his guard back up, Stone answered the phone while keeping his anger at bay. "Hello."

"I do believe we have a problem, Alpha Blaylock."

"Oh? And what problem would that be?" he asked cautiously.

"I have one of your packmates here. One Danielle Jones. Familiar with that name?"

Stone barely held the growl back when he spoke again. "Yes. I'll be there to get her shortly."

"That's where the problem lies, Alpha. I'm keeping her here for questioning."

"Why?" he asked the Sulphur Springs' alpha, worried the man was trying to give asylum to one of the people behind his mate's attack.

"Because she has just accused my daughter of being part of a scheme to kill your mate. And until I figure out if she's lying or not, her ass isn't going any-fucking-where."

Stone knew he would need to be careful about what he said next, so as to not escalate the situation too quickly, but there was something he needed to know.

"What will you do if you find out your daughter was involved in my mate's attack?"

"Exile her from the pack." His statement was sure and swift. Except, that wasn't the answer Stone had been hoping for.

"The punishment for attacking an alpha or his mate is death," he reminded the other man.

"Don't ask me to kill my own daughter."

"Are you so sure that she's guilty that you would need to worry about that?" Stone asked, trying to gauge the other man's frame of mind.

There was silence for a few seconds on the other end, but finally, the Sulphur Springs' alpha answered him. "Suspicious enough that I'm calling you first before heading the investigation myself, instead of just snapping your wolf's neck."

The line went dead, and Stone wished it hadn't. He had just been about to tell the man to go ahead and snap Danielle's neck, anyway.

Pushing that thought aside, he felt a sense of relief crash over him. He knew who had attacked his mate and some of the why, all because one old bitty had been prejudice against humans, and apparently didn't believe in mixing races. Hopefully, the Sulphur Springs' alpha would get the rest of the answers he needed shortly. Until then, he was going to do what he hadn't been able to do in months. He was going to go see his mate.

It had been so hard staying away from Dia to keep her safe. But when you loved someone, you made sacrifices for them. There was nothing he wouldn't do for his mate, and staying away had been paramount when he hadn't known why someone had attacked her parents' house and almost killed her. Now he knew the truth, and that the fact he had stayed away and told everyone she was dead had probably spared her life. There was no doubt in Stone's mind that, if Mrs. Jones had found out she was alive in that hospital, and pregnant, too, she would have gone there to try to kill Dia and the baby.

Now, barring what might happen with the Sulphur Springs pack, it was safe enough to bring his mate home, and there wasn't a thing in this world that could stop him from doing just that.

# *Chapter Thirteen*

Sneaking into the hospital was much trickier than he thought it would be. Then again, it was in the middle of the night, well after visiting hours. Nevertheless, Stone didn't care. He needed to see his mate, and he needed to see her now. That was why it was three o'clock in the morning, and he was sitting here, watching her sleep.

He wasn't going to wake her up, knowing she needed to rest. The chance to just sit here and watch her like this was all he needed.

His sweet Dia had changed so much since he had seen her last. Her hair had been cut short, and while he had loved it long, she was just as beautiful with the chopped strands. She looked healthy, with creamy skin and pink cheeks, although he could tell she had lost a little bit of weight.

The thing he couldn't take his eyes off, though, was the small baby bump underneath the blanket. That was their cub lying safely in his mother's womb.

And there was no doubt for Stone that it would be a boy, because his family had not birthed a daughter in their line since as long as it could be traced on the family tree. Hundreds of years.

He couldn't wait to see Dia more round with their child. Her breasts heavy with milk. She didn't know it yet, but he hoped they would have many children together. Stone had hated being an only child and didn't want that for his child.

If he was honest with himself, it was also because of the baby making process. What red-blooded male didn't want to touch and taste their mate as often as possible?

When Dia started to stir, Stone was aware of every small movement she made. He could tell she was waking up, and for the first time in his life, he was truly worried, knowing she wouldn't remember him. Therefore, he stayed in his chair instead of rushing to her side, and waited for her to slowly wake up.

It took her a few minutes as her body fought her mind to wake up. She tossed and turned, ending up on her side, facing him, making him the first thing Dia saw when she opened her eyes.

She gasped in shock, and he felt horrible for scaring her, but he didn't move a muscle. The best thing he could do right then was to remain as calm and soothing to her as possible.

"Who are you?" Dia asked with a nervous voice.

How little did she know that those words cut like a knife through his soul.

Stone knew she couldn't help it, but still, some part of him had hoped she would take one look at him and remember everything. Regardless, he had already thought of the best way to answer this question on his way over here, just in case she didn't remember him.

"I'm your husband."

Confused, she started to shake her head. "You have to be joking. I've been here for over two months. If you were my husband, you would have been here by now. They would have been able to find you in records and contacted you."

Stone shook his head. "We didn't get a chance to file the marriage certificate yet. I had to leave for my job, and you wanted to tell your parents in person that we had gotten married before we did it."

Dia's eyebrows scrunched down. She looked as if she were thinking too hard.

A silent moment passed between them before she finally said, "We got married and didn't have my parents there? Why would I do that?"

At this question, Stone gave her a smile. He knew it probably looked like a sad smile to her, but he couldn't help grinning at the memories of his courting her.

"This is going to sound unbelievable, but you could say we had one of those 'love at first sight' relationships. We didn't know each other very long before we got married, but that was because we love each other so damn much."

She looked surprised at his answer. "Are you telling me we had some whirlwind romance?"

Stone nodded, then pointed at her belly. "I didn't even know you were pregnant when you went to see your parents."

Bringing her hand up to her forehead, Dia started to rub it as a look of pain crossed her face.

"Dia, are you okay?"

She shook her head. "My head is starting to hurt really bad."

At those words, Stone jumped out of his chair and rushed to her side. It was his natural instinct to protect his mate. Unfortunately, his mate didn't remember that she was his mate, and the move scared her.

Dia scooched back in her bed and held the hand that had been rubbing her forehead up to stop him. "Please don't come any closer."

Stone help up both of his hands to show her he meant her no harm. "Sorry, I just wanted to make sure you were okay. I'm a bit on edge from coming here and seeing you in the hospital for the first time. I'm sorry it took me so long to find out, Dia."

She started rubbing her forehead again while squinting her tired eyes. "Can you please leave?" Dia asked hesitantly. Then, with a stronger voice, she added, "I just can't deal with this right now with the way my head is starting to hurt."

He took another step back and let his arms drop to his sides. Leaving would kill him, but he didn't want to cause any harm to his mate, either.

"Would you like me to get the nurse on the way out?"

She shook her head. "I just want to go back to sleep."

He took a sideways step toward the door, then asked her, "Can I come back later?"

This time, it was Dia who dropped her hand as she gave him a suspicious look. Slowly, enunciating every word, she said, "I won't be here later. I'm being moved."

"Can you tell me where you're going so I can visit you there, then?"

Dia nibbled on her bottom lip as she thought.

"How do I know you're not some crazy person?"

Good question. He was almost proud of her for asking it.

"How about I prove it to you until you can remember me? Let me visit you, and we can talk about our life together."

She shook her head as another sharp pain hit it. "Please just go."

Stone walked out of the room with the knowledge he had left his heart behind him. It killed him to do it after he'd had grand daydreams that she would remember who he was and come home with him, but life didn't always work out the way you wanted it to.

He would just have to be patient and help his mate remember.

# *Chapter Fourteen*

*One week later…*

Stone sat in the cab of his truck, staring at the women's home that his mate was currently residing in. He had come to despise looking at the place, and not because there was anything wrong with it. On the contrary, it was a nice place set in the country. He imagined it was very peaceful there for the women who had made this their haven.

No, he despised the Fresh Start Women's Center because his mate was living in it, and not at home with him. For an entire week, he had come here every day, knocking at the door and asking to see Dia. And for seven days straight, he had been turned away with one simple statement: "She's not ready to see you."

He wanted to roar at those words. He wanted to shout at the top of his lungs, "Tough shit because I'm coming in, anyway!" Both of those were things he could not do.

Taking a deep breath, he said a silent prayer that today would be the day that his mate came to her senses and took a chance at seeing him. Stone had convinced himself that the night in the hospital, the reason Dia had gotten that headache, was because some part of her subconscious mind knew him and was trying to make her remember. If only he could see her again, she might remember everything … or at least him. However, the stubborn woman kept refusing to see him.

Stone was just about to get out of his truck when his cell phone started ringing. Looking at the screen, he recognized the number as the alpha of Sulphur Springs. They had unfinished business to take care of, and as much as he hated having to wait that much longer to go knock on the door, this really needed to be handled once and for all.

"Hello."

"Alpha Blaylock, I am calling to inform you that my daughter confessed to her crimes."

A little surprised, Stone asked, "Did she tell you where she got the magic from and why she was trying to kill my mate?"

A sad sigh crossed the line before the other man spoke again. "What I am about to tell you, I would appreciate it if you kept it to yourself."

"Depending on what you tell me, I'll do my best to honor that. But if I feel that my beta or alpha female need to know, I will tell them."

"Which is something I understand all too well." There was another sigh before the man confessed,

"My daughter was born from a one-night stand I had with a witch. She seduced me with one of her spells, casting it to make me believe she was my mate. I didn't figure out until after she was pregnant that she wasn't truly my mate. By then, it was too late. I've kept my daughter's magic a secret up until now to protect her. What I didn't realize was that I would need to protect others from her, too."

"Well, that explains how she got the magic, but what you haven't explained is why she tried to kill my mate."

There was silence on the other end for a short time, and then the alpha's grief-clogged voice came through the line. "I didn't get an answer directly from her before she was killed by another wolf."

"Who killed your daughter and why?"

"It was Danielle. She thought that, by killing my daughter, she was protecting her great-grandmother somehow."

"It's too late for that. Her great-grandmother killed herself instead of answering any more of my questions."

This time, a frustrated sigh came from the other man. "Then it seems that we'll never know why my daughter did it, since my daughter cast a spell on Danielle just before she died, turning her into a rat.

The little bitch scurried away from us the moment she realized what she had become."

Stone heaved a sigh of relief. "It's done, then."

"It's done," the Sulphur Springs' alpha agreed. "I apologize for my daughter's involvement and hope this will not affect the alliance we have."

What was that old adage? Keep your friends close and your enemies closer? The Sulphur Springs' alpha had done the right thing, but Stone didn't know if he would ever be able to trust him the same way again. Therefore, it would be wiser to keep the alliance intact so he could keep a closer eye on the man.

"The alliance is still intact, but I would like to know now if there are any more magic-wielding shifters you're hiding."

"None," the other man said. His voice sounded truthful, but Stone would be wary of that pack from here on out.

After the two men hung up, Stone sat silently in his truck for a few moments. He couldn't imagine how hard that must have been for the other man, to interrogate and prosecute his own daughter like that. Not only had the man just lost his daughter, he had just given Stone some pretty powerful ammo to use against him if he had wanted to make a war out of this. Stone could only find himself grateful that the man had done the right thing.

It was hard to believe that after months of worrying and missing his mate, that it was all over. Now he could give one hundred percent of his attention to wooing his mate back into his arms.

Getting out of the truck, he slowly made his way to the front door and knocked. The door opened, and the same woman who had turned him away for the seven days prior was there at the door. His heart sank that this would be the same.

"I would like to see Dia please."

The woman gave him a sad look. "I'm sorry, but she says she's still not ready to see you."

Stone swallowed his pride and gave the woman he loved what she needed—space from him.

Nodding, he turned and walked away, heading for his truck. Hopefully tomorrow would have a different outcome.

Jessie Lane

# *Chapter Fifteen*

*One week later…*

"He's back again, Dia," Charlotte, the woman who ran the Fresh Start Women's Center, told her.

Damn, the man was persistent. But maybe that was because he had told her the truth that day in the hospital and he really was her husband. She couldn't think of any other reason why a man would come every day for two weeks straight, only to be turned away at the door, time and time again.

Charlotte looked back at Dia from the window at the front of the house and said, "Maybe you should talk to him this time."

"Maybe I should." She sighed. "He certainly doesn't listen to directions very well."

Yesterday, she'd had Charlotte tell him she needed more time and to give her at least a week before he came back again.

Dia got up from where she was sitting on the couch when she heard Charlotte mutter, "What's he doing?" Two seconds later Charlotte said, "Come look, Dia. He has a sign!"

She picked up her pace until she was standing next to Charlotte, looking out the large bay window.

There he stood in the grass, wearing jeans; a white, long-sleeved shirt; and a beanie on his head with a big white sign that said in bold, black letters: "As you wish, princess."

The feeling of a million bricks crashing down on her brain totally overwhelmed her. Dia had to put her forehead against the window as she cried out in pain. Subconsciously, she could hear the other women in the house running toward her, asking if she was okay. Dia even heard the front door next to her slamming open and shouts of fear from the women surrounding her as the man who claimed to be her husband stormed into the house, demanding to see her. None of it was enough to stop the barrage of memories that crashed into her mind like a Mack truck on steroids.

It was like a movie on fast forward as bits of her life flashed before her eyes. Her parents. Her twelfth birthday when they gave her a brand-new bicycle. Going to cosmetology school, and then mentoring under Betty Anne.

Last but not least were the memories of her would-be husband, who she knew had lied about who he was to her but not his name. Stone was her mate, not her husband. And she immediately understood why he had to tell her that lie. Because she was a human mated to a wolf shifter.

Most importantly, Dia knew there was one very important fact that he had not lied about: he loved her. She knew that with every fiber of her being now, and hated that she had forgotten about his love for even a minute. The thought brought a new wave of tears on.

Dia and her baby were not truly alone anymore. She had some of her memories back, and now she had Stone. They were going to be a family, and she would never have to feel the crushing emotion of that loneliness again.

Ignoring all the others around her, Dia threw herself in Stone's direction and wrapped her arms around his neck.

He hugged her tight to his body and rocked her back and forth in a soothing motion. "Shhh, it's okay, princess; I've got you."

With emotion clogging her throat, tears rolling down her face, and their baby pressing against them, Dia said the only thing that came to mind.

"I'm not a fucking princess."

Jessie Lane

# *Chapter Sixteen*

*One week later...*

Dia wasn't sure if it was pregnancy hormones, but she was about to give in to the urge to hit her mate over the head with a frying pan.

For an entire week, Stone had been babying her and treating her as if she were fragile glass. It was nice at first to be pampered, but it got old really quick.

The man wouldn't even let her take a shower by herself, which would be fine if they were having sexy fun times in the shower, but they weren't. It was because he was afraid she was going to slip and hit her head, and according to Stone, he never, ever wanted Dia to forget who he was ever again.

Then there was the food. My God, the man kept trying to shove food in her face.

"You're eating for two," he would say. Well, with the way he was trying to feed her twenty times a day, one might think she was eating for a whole flippin' football team.

Last, but certainly not least, was the sex ... Or lack of it.

Her mate had not made love to her since she remembered who he was. It was like he was afraid to touch her. Afraid that the smallest wrong move would somehow cause her to lose her memory all over again. She couldn't keep living like this.

And besides irrational anger, the other thing pregnancy hormones seemed to do was make her horny. She felt like a cat in heat, and her mate wouldn't soothe the constant ache she carried around these days.

This just wouldn't do. So, Dia decided something drastic needed to be done. She needed to seduce her mate.

That was why, at four o'clock in the morning, she was wide awake, staring at him, trying to decide the best way to plan her move. And as she laid there and plotted, Stone rolled over to his back, and she watched in fascination as his erect dick tented the sheet.

Apparently, she wasn't the only one who was horny. That made her decision of what she was going to do next so much easier.

Slowly, so as to not wake him, Dia pulled the sheet down his body until it cleared his knees and his proud erection stood tall in the air. Then she quietly made her way between his legs and placed her hands on the bed on either side of his hips. This left her hovering over the part of him she was practically drooling for. She then bent her head forward and gave his length a long, soft lick.

Stone moaned in his sleep at the touch. She loved the way her mate moaned, so she licked him again, continuing the long, slow licks, tracing the slit of his head, teasing him in his sleep. His hips jerked a little here and there at her touches, but Stone had yet to wake up.

Dia had tasted every part of his length when she finally took him whole into her mouth and began to suck. She loved the softness of his skin as she moved her mouth up and down his shaft. Adding her hand to the base of his cock, she gave a little squeeze and heard Stone's breath hitch in response. Dia knew now her mate was awake.

"Fuck, princess, what are you doing to me?"

Dia pulled her mouth off his dick so she could answer his question. "Loving you. I need you, Stone."

Sliding up his body, she rubbed her core across his length, teasing herself with the rocking motion. Then Dia put one hand on his chest for support as she slid over and over again, hitting her clit and driving her need higher. For the first time, she could feel the sexual changes that pregnancy had brought in her. The fullness and sensitivity to her breasts, and the way her clit felt like it was on a hair trigger.

"If you're gonna do something with that, sweetheart, you need to hurry up. I'm about to blow."

She moaned as Stone ran his hands up her body, over her belly, and then farther up still to cup her breasts in his hands, teasing her nipples with the pad of his thumbs. Dia was soaking now with want, and he was the only one who could fill her needs.

Rocking her body upward a little, she let the head of his cock slide to her opening, and then slowly started to sit down on it. Her mate's hands moved to her hips to help steady her, but at least he wasn't stopping her.

"Son of a bitch, that feels so good."

Dia paused when she was filled with him, enjoying the sensation and squeezing her inner walls around his length. There was no pain or anything else that implied she needed to slow down, so she lifted up, and then sat down on his length hard again, setting the tempo for how she wanted to take her mate. Fully, as if she were as much an animal as he was.

She rose and fell, increasing her tempo until all she could feel was that edge of pleasure. On the precipice of falling over into ecstasy, it seemed Stone was right there with her. He held on to her a little tighter with his hands, helping to lift her, then slamming her down on his length as he started to lose control. Dia didn't mind the help at all as her body tensed up, her orgasm coming, making her limbs twitch erratically.

"Fuck, I can feel you squeezing me," he panted out as he lifted her up, then let her fall on his length again.

"Please, Stone, please," Dia started to beg, unable to put into words what she needed.

"I've got you, baby. Just hold on to me." With that, Stone sat up, then rolled them both until he was now on top of her, making sure to put space between their bodies so she wouldn't feel crushed. Then he buried his face in her neck.

"Bite me, love," Dia panted out. "Give me another mating mark. Remind me what it's like to feel like I'm totally yours."

"Mine," Stone growled against her neck.

"Yes, yours," she breathed back.

One thrust after another, she took his thick cock into her body, loving the way he took control and made them both feel good.

Dia started to think there was no way she could ever feel better than this, but then Stone ran the edge of his fangs over her neck, teasing her with the hint of what was to come.

"Please!"

"I love the way you beg, mate."

"I'll beg all you want," she panted back, "as long as you make love to me like this from now on. Please, Stone, don't push me away again."

"Never," he growled against her skin before piercing his teeth on the spot where her neck met her shoulder.

The flash of pain sent her over the edge and into that euphoric place of pleasure that only he could take her.

Stone's hips started to jerk erratically before he filled her with his seed, making her burn from the inside out. Then Dia was running her hand over his sweaty back, petting him lovingly as they both came down from their sexual haze.

Eventually, Stone pulled back enough to look her in the face and asked, "Did you really feel as though I was pulling away from you, love?"

Biting her bottom lip nervously, she nodded, not knowing what to say. How did one tell their mate that, because they didn't seem to want to be intimate with the other, they felt bereft of love and attention?

He, on the other hand, wasn't at a loss for words.

Stone shook his head. "I'm so sorry, princess. I promise that's not what I meant to do. I'm just so scared of losing you again that the wolf and I felt the need to be careful with you. With my shifter strength, and you being a human, I was afraid I might get too rough with you, with as badly as both the wolf and I want you. I promise I've wanted to be inside you, wrapped around you, from the moment I had you back in my arms."

"No more ignoring this? Because I need your love in all ways, Stone."

He shook his head again. "No more, mate."

With that, he kissed her sweetly, showing her how much he loved her with his lips and tongue before tucking her up against his body so they could both go back to sleep.

It was the first time that Dia had a truly peaceful slumber since she had come home.

# *Epilogue*

"Do you know what you're having?"

Since Dia was currently going through another contraction that felt like someone was stabbing her in the back, she wasn't exactly in the mood to have idle chitchat with the nurse. That didn't stop her from telling the lady the truth.

"Yeah, a fucking bowling ball. Now get him the hell out!"

The nurse clucked her tongue while Stone wiped her sweaty brow with a cloth.

"Now, now, dear, it can't be that bad. Millions of women have given birth before you. You're going to be just fine."

Dia growled, "Says the lady with her hand up my woo-ha. How about you get it out of there so I can push this kid out?"

The nurse poked and prodded a few seconds more then removed her hand. "You're at ten centimeters, Mrs. Blaylock!" she chirped with a huge smile on her face. "It's time to get the doctor and have a baby."

"That's what I've been trying to tell you!" Dia wailed as yet another contraction racked her body.

The nurse left the room, and Stone grabbed her hand, bringing it to his mouth to kiss. "I love you, mate." The sincere words melted her heart and took her mind off the pain for a few seconds.

"I love you, too, Stone, but if you ever knock me up again, I'm cutting your dick off!"

The nervous alpha was smart enough not to answer his mate while she was cranky and in pain. Instead, he stood there, lending her his silent strength.

Just then, the nurse came back into the room with a doctor and two other nurses in tow.

As happy as Dia was that she was finally going to be able to hold her baby in her arms, she wanted to strangle all the happy people in the room. Did they not see she was in a shit ton of pain here?

The doctor pulled a stool up to the end of her hospital bed and sat down, practically disappearing between her bent and spread legs. "Next contraction, I want you to push, Mrs. Blaylock."

She pushed, and then she pushed some more. In fact, Dia pushed for half an hour before their baby was finally born, free of her body.

Happiness and love surged through her in a wave so strong, she would have collapsed had she already not been lying down. And then the doctor said the three most magical words Dia thought she would ever hear.

"It's a girl!"

Dia gasped in delight, then looked over at her mate, who looked like he had been knocked silly. "Isn't that wonderful, Stone? We have a little girl!"

"But we Blaylocks always have boys," he uttered in surprise.

"Not anymore!" Dia crowed happily. Truly, she wouldn't have cared if they'd had a boy, but the thought of a sweet, little girl was like icing on the cake. She could already imagine how their daughter would be. Dia's sass and all her daddy's alpha confidence. The world wouldn't know what knocked them on their asses.

Sort of like her daughter's father right now.

Holding her arms out, Dia told the nurse who was weighing their baby, "Hand her over. I want to meet my daughter." It wasn't a very nice way to demand her daughter, but it was better than the "Gimme" she had really wanted to say.

The nurse handed her over with a smile on her face. Dia didn't mind the smile now. Hell, she probably had the biggest one in the room.

In that moment, as she looked down upon their child, everything in the world was perfect, especially her baby girl.

Dia then looked over at Stone, who was staring at both her and the baby with tears in his eyes. She nodded for him to come closer, and as he did, he asked her, "What will we name her, my love?"

She didn't have to think about it; Dia already knew.

"Betty. Because if Betty Ann had never talked me into buying her shop, I would have never met you."

He nodded as he stared at their daughter some more, the yearning to hold her in his eyes.

Supporting Betty's head, Dia held her out to Stone. "Hold her, honey. Say hello to the newest member of our family."

The doctor and nurses disappeared for a few moments to give them time with their daughter as Stone picked her tiny, little body up in his giant hands. Cradling her in his arms, he rocked his body back and forth while staring at their daughter as if he were trying to imprint her every little feature to memory. Dia would know, because she had done the same.

The baby already had her strawberry blonde hair, but Dia was hoping she would end up with Stone's gorgeous eyes. She watched as her mate dipped his head and inhaled deeply, memorizing Betty's scent. When he was done, he placed a kiss on her tiny, little head just before Betty started fussing.

"What is it, little one? You want your mom?" He used a finger to smooth it over her cap of baby fine hair, and then whispered possibly the sweetest thing Dia had ever heard him say as he handed Betty back to her, "As you wish, princess."

# Note from the Author

Thank you for reading *The Alpha's Secret Family*! You're the absolute best for giving little ol' me a chance. For every Indie Author you read, somewhere out there a fairy gets its wings! Okay, maybe not, but it still seems pretty magical.

For those of you thinking, "That Sulphur Springs Alpha let Patty's granddaughter off too easily!" Lets just say that I write everything the way I do for a reason, and there's a very good chance you'll see those two in the near future.

I hope you enjoyed reading this book as much as I enjoyed writing it. If you did, please consider leaving a review at your favorite online retailers or review websites. These are great ways to help spread the word about books to readers who have yet to discover them.

Happy reading!

XoXo,

*Jessie Lane*

# About the Author

Jessie Lane is a best-selling author of Paranormal and Contemporary Romance, as well as, Upper YA Paranormal Romance/Fantasy.

She lives in Kentucky with her two little Rock Chicks in-the-making and her over protective alpha husband that she's pretty sure is a latent grizzly bear shifter. She has a passionate love for reading and writing naughty romance, cliff hanging suspense, and out-of-this-world characters that demand your attention, or threaten to slap you around until you do pay attention to them.

She's also a proud member of the Romance Writers of America (RWA).

**For more information on Jessie Lane:**

http://jessielanebooks.com

**Or you can send Jessie Lane an email at:**

jessie_lane@jessielanebooks1.com

# You May Also Like

# Howls Romance

## *Classic romance... with a furry twist!*

Did you enjoy this Howls Romance story?

**If YES, check out the other books in the Howls Romance line!**

Royal Dragon's Baby by Anya Nowlan

The Werewolf Tycoon's Baby by Celia Kyle

Pregnant with the Werelion King's Cub by Claire Pike

The Billionaire Shifter's Secret Baby by Diana Seere

The Werebear's Unwanted Bride by Marina Maddix

Hunted by the Dragon Duke by Mina Carter

CPSIA information can be obtained
at www.ICGtesting.com
Printed in the USA
LVOW11s1417081117
555504LV00001B/2/P